LOVE AND DESIRE AND HATE

All too often a once happily married couple wake up, look at each other and wonder if love has changed to hate. When divorce seems inevitable the chief sufferers are the children. In this absorbing novel, Denise Robins deals with this very problem, and pulls no punches.

By the same author

The Unlit Fire
The Untrodden Snow
The Noble One
Blaze of Love
Restless Heart
Slave Woman
Brief Ecstasy
Fever of Love
The Crash
Infatuation
Moment of Love
Lightning Strikes Twice
House of the Seventh Cross
Wait for Tomorrow
Laurence, My Love
Never Give All
Gay Defeat
The Cyprus Love Affair
Strange Meeting
Climb to the Stars
Gypsy Lover

and available in Hodder Paperbacks

Love and Desire and Hate

Denise Robins

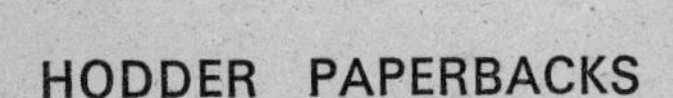

First printed 1969
Hodder Paperback Edition 1971

Printed in Great Britain
for Hodder Paperbacks Ltd.,
St Paul's House, Warwick Lane, London, E.C.4,
by Richard Clay (The Chaucer Press), Ltd.,
Bungay, Suffolk

ISBN 0 340 14877 2

1

THE Headmaster looked at the clock on his desk. Half-past twelve. Time to relax a bit. It was a warm sticky morning. He had had a lot of paper work, a rather trying staff conference, and an added aggravation because the senior matron had gone sick. It was the very devil these days trying to replace good staff. The Head was not in the best of humours although he was ordinarily a cheerful, just, and tolerant man. And this was one of the best and most successful Preparatory Schools in the South of England. He had nothing to complain about. But when a knock came on the door, he answered rather irritably:

"Oh, come in, come in!"

Who wanted him now? He had no more appointments as far as he could remember.

The door opened. A slim boy, rather small and slight for his twelve years; but good-looking, in a clean white shirt and grey flannel shorts, walked in. His arms were held rather stiffly at his side. He looked embarrassed.

The Headmaster relaxed.

"Ah, hello, Grifford. Come in, my boy. What can I do for you?"

"I just want to speak to you for a moment if I may, sir."

"Certainly, sit down."

The Head's good humour returned.

Peter Grifford was one of his best pupils, leaving at the end of this term to go on to his Public School and although not too good at games, he was a nice co-operative boy; had first-class brains too. The Classics master found him brilliant. Bit of a change. Most of the lads these days swarmed like inquisitive bees around Maths and Science. The Headmaster was a Classical scholar. Both he and his wife had a soft spot for young Grifford.

"What's troubling you?" he asked, and smiled at the boy.

Grifford sat down, pulling at his right ear, obviously nervous. But he had never been afraid of the Head. He blurted out:

"I've come on behalf of Butler, please sir."

Now the Headmaster pulled at his own ear.

"Butler? Oh, yes, Butler – in the Fifth?"

"Yes, sir."

"Well, I don't know why you've come about him Grifford. Can't he fight his own battles?"

Grifford coloured. He had the sort of fine pale skin that flushes easily. He'd be a nice-looker when he broadened out a bit, and put on a few inches, the Headmaster reflected. Good bone structure. Eyes perhaps a little too large and thickly lashed. Like his mother's, as far as the Headmaster could remember. He had a soft spot for her, too. Beautiful woman. He preferred her to the father. Mr. Grifford talked too much, and mostly about himself. Odd thing, but he never seemed as interested in his son as the mother was, and it was she who came to most of the school affairs; she who fetched the boy for his *exeats* and often brought him back, too. They were obviously very close, mother and son. The Headmaster actually preferred things the other way round. He liked the father–son partnership. Made a better man of the child, in his opinion.

Grifford said:

"Well, it's a bit awkward, sir. I know Butler ought to come and see you because he's been so awfully upset lately. He was in a bit of a tiz-waz this morning and when I said he ought to tell you himself what he was feeling, he said he'd rather I did it for him."

The Headmaster put the tips of his fingers together, leaned back in his chair and gave a faint amused smile.

"I see. So you are the carrier of the 'tiz-waz', whatever that may be."

Young Grifford blinked his long lashes and responded with a faint smile on his own lips.

"Yes, sir."

"Out with it, then."

"Well, sir, you know that Butler's parents are getting a

divorce and it's upset him frightfully. I know that he's done badly in form this last week or two and been getting into trouble for being rude to old Twittering . . . sorry sir, I mean Wittering . . ." Grifford's face was scarlet now. He cleared his throat and looked anywhere but at the Headmaster. He wished he had not come.

Oh God, said the Headmaster to himself, now I know what this is all about.

Of course he knew that a divorce was impending between Butler's parents. It worried and angered him. It was never good for the young when parents separated like that. He'd seen the harm done so many times; the inevitable repercussion on a sensitive boy; the rapid fall from grace, as Grifford already suggested. Bad marks. General deterioration in character. Only for a time, perhaps. They pulled out of it eventually, but it was bad while it lasted. Damned selfish, these couples who went their own ways without any consideration for the kids. Far too many of them doing it now, too. There was the case of that boy, who had come from a broken home, behaved so badly at school, the Head had to ask the wretched mother to remove him.

He hoped this wouldn't be the case with Butler. He was a splendid little fellow. Six months younger than Grifford. Not as intelligent, but first-rate at sports.

The father had come down personally to tell the Head that the home was breaking up. The mother wanted to go off with some other chap. The Head remembered listening to a long rigmarole about the domestic wrangles, etc., that had led up to the débâcle. Mr. Butler had, as a matter of fact, struck him as being a bit sticky and awkward, and at the end of the conversation he had even felt a faint pity for the erring Mrs. Butler. But most of his compassion went to the boy.

"What's Butler got to say then, Grifford?" he asked with some unease.

"He asked me to ask you, sir, if you'd write to his parents and beg them not to get divorced. He's very fond of them both, sir, and he's keen on his home. He says he feels sure you could persuade them to stay together."

"He flatters me," said the Headmaster sadly, "I don't think

I could possibly achieve any such thing. I told Mr Butler what I thought about it when I saw him but it didn't have any effect. Anyhow, it seems that it is the mother who is leaving home."

"Yes, sir, but Butler says she hasn't left yet and it's all still a bit uncertain," said young Grifford eagerly, "and he says it'll be so awful if he goes home for the summer hols and has his aunt there instead of his mother."

Oh God! thought the Headmaster again.

"Please, sir, couldn't you do anything?"

"Well, it's very decent of you to have come along and made this appeal on your friend's behalf, but I really can't interfere, you know, Grifford. It's not my business."

"It means an awful lot to Butler, sir. He doesn't like his aunt."

"Look, Grifford, you've got to face up to hard facts in this life and not let feelings run away with you. What I mean is, life does crack down on one now and again and deals some heavy blows, but one has to stand up to them. Poor old Butler's got to face *his* troubles. I don't suppose you know much about this sort of thing because you come from a happy home but it may well be better for Butler in the long run once his mother has gone. No doubt he'll be visiting her regularly and from what I've gathered there've been some pretty hectic scenes and rows going on in the home. Don't you think Butler might find it more peaceful once the divorce is over, and accepts the change?"

"No, I don't, sir," said Grifford.

For the third time the Headmaster muttered: *Oh God!* to himself. He heartily agreed with Grifford.

"You see, sir," said Grifford, "Butler also asked me to ask you to tell his people that he doesn't mind about the rows, no matter how grim they are. He'd rather listen to them and keep both his parents. He says so."

The Headmaster suddenly felt old and tired. He sat silent, playing with the pen on his blotter, thanking God for his own happy marriage and wishing that he could have helped young Butler, but after the conversation he had had with the father he didn't see the slightest use in even passing on that sad, sad message. So the boy would rather listen to the rows, and keep his home and parents intact. Poor little brute!

Now suddenly Grifford made a startling announcement.

"I know what Butler feels, sir, because things are not always all right between my own parents."

"Oh dear, Grifford – I never thought . . . surely not . . ."

The Head found himself stammering and a sensation of very real concern for this, one of his favourite pupils, turned the Headmaster's thoughts from the other boy.

Grifford appeared to have overcome his nerves and enlightened the Head still further.

"Mum and I are terrific friends and Dad's often terrific too, of course, but he and Mum are not at all alike and I hear arguments that I don't suppose they think I hear. Mum's very quiet but Dad goes right up in the air when he's put out. I'm only telling you this, sir, because when I talked to Butler about the divorce I thought how much I'd hate it if my parents had one."

"Of course, of course," said the Headmaster, and rose to his feet, "but they're not going to have a divorce. There are always . . . ahem . . ." he coughed "little matrimonial differences of opinion, you know. It's only to be expected over the years . . . ahem . . . but I'm sure you've nothing to worry about, Grifford."

"Oh, no, but I just wanted to say that knowing what I would feel, I hoped you'd try and help Butler."

Now the Head smiled very kindly at the boy who had been here in the school for the last four years and been a credit to it. He was going to miss him.

"I'll do what I can, Grifford. As a matter of fact I think I'll send Butler's exact words to his mother, today. You never know, it might do some good. And thanks for coming. It was very decent of you."

"Thank you, sir," said Grifford, and left the room with an air of relief.

The Headmaster put a hand into a drawer of his desk and pulled out a pipe which he fingered thoughtfully. The conversation with young Grifford had depressed him not a little.

It was obvious that Butler was feeling wretched even before his mother had left home. A pity the boy knew, perhaps. But nothing was hidden from these young people today. Nothing.

The Head sat down in his revolving chair and started to fill his pipe. But curiously enough it was not the memory of Butler and his miseries that weighed on his mind. It was that unexpected admission from young Grifford that his own parents did not get on too well, that troubled the Headmaster. He wouldn't like to think that there was going to be trouble *there*. It would be very bad for Peter Grifford, indeed.

What had happened? They were always charmed by Mrs. Grifford when she came to the school. She was intelligent, and sensible about her son. He'd noticed that. Not the type to be ringing up, for ever complaining, or asking about her little darling. She was exactly the right type of mother. It *couldn't*, surely, be her fault if there was trouble in the Grifford home. Much more likely to be that smooth, handsome, garrulous fellow she'd married.

"Who's to know?" the Head asked himself aloud. "Who the *heck's* to know? One seldom sees people on the outside as they really are, in their own home."

He lit his pipe and sat back smoking, brooding and, if he cared to admit it, worrying.

2

WHENEVER Frances Grifford received a telephone call from her mother-in-law beginning with "Oh, Fran, please come down and see me at once, dear", she knew what it meant. These summonses came regularly. Mrs. Grifford had had another dust-up with somebody in the hotel and wanted a change.

She had actually stayed at this present one in Eastbourne longer than at most. She had moved from one hotel to another at least six times during the last five years since her husband's death.

Fran found her trying but because she was Rodney's mother and Fran had a kind heart, she usually did her best to help.

Rodney was the one who complained. Mama to him had become an old nuisance but Fran argued:

"The poor old thing's lonely and helpless, and she's been rather confused since your father died. You don't understand her."

Rodney's reply to that was:

"You can be an angel if you want, darling, I never was one and I've no time."

Typical of Rodney. He rarely had time for anybody but himself. He was really very fond of his mother but managed to wriggle out of most of his disagreeable responsibilities. What had he to grumble at, Fran often asked herself. When his father died, in order to save death duties, he had left everything to Rodney. All he had to do was to make his mother a reasonable allowance which of course he did. That, he didn't begrudge her. Both his parents had been very good to him. When he left Cambridge he was lucky enough to be able to go straight into the firm of stockbrokers of which his father was once a senior partner. Since then Rodney, himself, had become a partner, and despite the recent squeeze and economic uncertainty, he was still able to make money. He had charm, good looks, and a good business brain.

On her way down to Eastbourne to see her mother-in-law, Fran thought, as she so often did, of her husband. She still felt much of the fervent love she had given him when they were first married, without, perhaps, all the illusions. She knew well that under all his charm there was another Rodney – a moody, and at times difficult, self-centred man. But then, as he had once told her, why try to preserve illusions? You always lose them. Better to be an intelligent realist, rather than a romantic fool.

"I know I'm a stinker, but go on loving me, Fran," he added – which she did, and she would think:

I expect he finds my adoration boring. Men don't really like to be adored and I'm not very clever with Rod. I don't think, anyhow, that he likes the me I really am, and the fact that I am romantic at heart.

Things change. They had both changed.

They had met fourteen years ago on the ski-slopes in Zürs – both of them good skiers. She, three months away from her coming-of-age, and he, four years older. He was gay and handsome; all the women looked at him and he had a way of looking back which they found irresistible. Fran was no exception. But her own success with him had staggered her, because she was a little shy and retiring and imagined Rodney Grifford would pass her by for a more dashing, sophisticated type of girl. Not at all. Before that holiday ended he appeared to be head over ears in love with her and she couldn't think about anything or anybody else. He was the first one she had ever cared for seriously. He said the same about her. There had been a lot of women already in young Rodney's life but with Fran, he said, it was different.

She used to be small and slender in those days, with rather fragile bones, and an elfin beauty; pointed chin, large eyes, and boyishly short dark hair cut with a fringe. Those were the days, too, when she adored dancing and he seemed just as keen about it. They danced every night, most of the night. They sat up at the bar drinking together. They went up the mountains in the sunshine for long excursions. They seemed to have a lot in common.

Seemed . . . that was the operative word Fran thought sadly as she drove through Caterham toward the coast on this fine September day.

Why was it that years of marriage, and habit and custom, and all the set-backs and frustrations, should so completely change the pattern of love – and the tune?

She didn't love Rod any less. At times she felt she loved him more. She was the faithful kind. A one-man girl. But she had an idea that he didn't feel the same way about her. Just an idea, nothing tangible. And after all, he told her openly, bluntly, a dozen times that she was too romantic and expected too much of him. So she tried to be different. And she no longer let him know how she felt. But it certainly seemed to her that the sort of women who attracted him today were not in the least like the Fran he had fallen for so madly at Zürs. They were more sophisticated.

Sophistication was something that Fran had never possessed nor was ever likely to. It wasn't in her make-up. She was really a domesticated 'stay-at-home' girl.

But they led a gay life, constantly entertaining in their small elegant house just off Eaton Square. She led it because *he* liked it. She had been trying for years to get him to the country, and even after their son, Peter, was born and she had pleaded that it was so much better for a child to live in the country, he had refused to move.

"Frannie, my *darling*, you know I'm not the type to want to mow a lawn or prune a rose. For God's sake don't try and turn me into one of that kind . . ."

That's what he said, so she stopped trying. But she just wondered why it never entered his head to make a single sacrifice for *her*.

He was at times affectionate. He brought her flowers and he gave her handsome presents when he was doing well, and everybody told her that she had a gorgeous husband and that she was lucky. On the whole, of course, she believed that she was lucky. She could never care for or live with anybody but Rod.

She wrote long letters at intervals to her father, who had married again after her mother died and settled in South Africa with his new wife, and told him how happy she was. But things *had* changed. And not even Fran with all her faith, her loyalty, her love, could deny that, after Miranda died. Miranda, the little daughter who had been born to them when Peter was three.

Fran rarely allowed herself to think about Miranda.

It was too terrible, and even though it was all past history the awful memory of the fatality that had happened eight years ago, could, if she allowed it, hit her like a physical blow.

Rod had never taken much interest in Peter. Children were not in his line and he had had a family only to please her. She knew and appreciated that fact. To Rod they were a bore. All too often one had to make sacrifices, financial or otherwise, for them. They might come between Rodney and his fun and freedom. He had been pleased when Fran, reluctantly, agreed to have a Nanny for Peter, and do the cooking herself, since they could not afford two living-in staff. Even today when Peter was more of a companionable age for Rodney, he shirked his paternal responsibilities. He was only mildly interested in the boy's progress and quite proud of him when he did well. He took him to rugger matches, or a circus, or any amusement only when it suited him.

But when Miranda was born it was different.

Suddenly all that was warm and affectionate in Rodney sprang to life, just as it had sprung when he first met Fran. He became the doting father.

Miranda was an enchanting little thing with big blue eyes like his, his thick fair hair and a way of looking at him out of the corners of those eyes that made him slap his leg and roar with laughter.

"God! She's me all over again – look at her, Fran. She'll be a smasher in her teens . . ."

When he came back from the office he never minded giving up an hour to Miranda. He sat with her, played with her, and allowed Fran, rather jealously, to give some extra love and attention to the thin, slight, serious-eyed little boy who kept in the background.

But during the two years of Miranda's lifetime Fran was really happy. Rodney became much more of the family man and even decided to buy a country cottage for weekends.

Then came that awful day when they went down to Gerrards Cross to look at a small place they had seen advertised.

They took both the children with them but not the Nanny. It was her day off. But Rodney would not go without Miranda and Fran thought it would be good for Peter to get some country air even for an hour or two.

The cottage they fancied was empty. It had a charming garden and a lily pond full of tangled weeds and one or two big waxen-creamy water-lilies.

It was a Saturday morning, and warm. Rodney decided that he must go round the corner to The Bull and get a pint of beer.

"I'll bring the children back some lemonade and whatever you fancy, darling," he said to Fran.

She smiled and waved – she was in good spirits and she had fallen in love with the cottage. Rod seemed in the mood to make an offer for it. He liked it, too.

Sometimes when Fran reconstructed in her mind the nightmare that followed, she wondered how it had *ever* happened. How she could ever have acted as she did, and not foreseen the possibility of a tragic accident. It had taken place just within a few minutes. *Just those few minutes* – between life and death.

She had left her cigarettes and matches in one of the upstairs bedrooms.

"I must run up and get my cigs, Pete," she said to the little boy. "Hold on to Miranda's hand and sit there just for a moment."

She left the two on the stone terrace in the sunlight, playing with one of Pete's new matchbox cars.

When she came down with the lighted cigarette between her lips, she was humming. The humming stopped as she saw neither Pete nor Miranda. Sharply she called to them. Pete came running, his hands cupped together and a look of excitement on his small face.

"I've caught a beekle . . . look, Mummy . . . I've caught a beekle."

"Where's Miranda?" she asked him.

"Don't know," he said, and returned to the enraptured scrutiny of the beetle struggling between his sticky fingers.

She found Miranda face downwards in the pond. In one small hand she still clutched a water-lily. It was quite obvious that she had tumbled in trying to grasp it. Pete was too young to realise what he did when he left her. Fran dragged the drowned little body out of the water and tried desperately to revive the child with the kiss of life; every nerve in her body screaming although she could not utter a sound, she was so shocked and stricken. Afterwards, of course, she blamed herself. She couldn't blame a four-year-old boy. *She* should not have gone upstairs and left them even for those few minutes.

What happened when Rodney came back from The Bull with the drinks she did not care to remember. Even after eight long years it pierced her heart like a knife to recall how he had gone to pieces and sobbed uncontrollably over the body of his idolised little daughter, while she ran – quite in vain – to fetch a doctor.

Of course, the time came when he turned on her – mad with grief.

"Why the hell did you leave her when you knew there was water there? What were you thinking of? You must have been out of your mind."

She did not bother to excuse herself. Numbed and anguished she admitted her guilt, feeling like a murderess even though she would have given her life to have prevented such a terrible thing from happening.

Of course, Rodney had regretted turning on her and that night they sobbed out their grief in each other's arms. He could not have been more kind. After the funeral he never mentioned Miranda's name again, neither did he allow a single photograph of her to be shown in the house. The loss of the baby girl had hit him hard. Fran knew that perhaps he had loved her more than he had ever loved anybody else in his life.

In time they both recovered, but Fran's feeling of guilt came back to torture her now and again. In her heart she believed that Rod had never really forgiven her because she had allowed Miranda to walk into that pond.

Never again, from that day to this, was there another suggestion that they should have a weekend cottage. Rod was finished with the country for good and all. And if she hoped that in his grief and loss he might turn more to his son, she was disappointed. It seemed to her that her strange husband became even more self-centred and less interested in Pete – or indeed in her.

But this was a pain that she had to learn to live with and never mention to a living soul.

3

"YOU'RE looking a bit peaky, aren't you, dear?"

Fran avoided looking straight at Rodney's mother.

"Oh, I don't know. It's a warm day and I found it close driving down from town. I'm fine really, Mama."

"I don't think you'd say so if you weren't," Mrs. Grifford muttered more to herself than to her daughter-in-law.

They had just finished lunch. They were sitting in the glass-covered verandah of the small hotel facing the sea-front. During the meal, Fran had hardly spoken, except to say 'yes', 'no', or 'really'. Mrs. Grifford did all the talking and had a string of complaints. But after all, that was what she had come for, Fran thought, and listened patiently.

The management here were putting the prices up; something about S.E.T. which Mrs. Grifford didn't understand, so Fran had to explain. She suspected the chamber-maid of taking her sweets. She kept a box of chocolates in her drawer and often forgot to lock it up and yesterday she had found half the sweets gone. She didn't like to accuse the girl openly and wondered if Fran would speak to the manageress. But Fran wriggled out of this by saying that she thought it would be tactless to do so if Mama meant to go on living there. Then with a sinking heart she had heard Mama threaten to pack up and go to another hotel. That would make the seventh move since Mr. Grifford died. Poor restless old thing! Fran looked at her with pity and the sort of affection that one feels for left-alone elderly people who have nothing to look forward to, and seem to want to add to their miseries by moaning about lost glories.

Mrs. Grifford had grown stout and at seventy-six looked more than her age. Fran could see no resemblance to the good-looking woman in the painting which Rodney's father had commissioned and which now hung in Fran's dining-room. The once thick fair hair that Rod had inherited was sparse and grey, and she would have it set in horrid little waves. The fair complexion of her youth had reddened and grown coarse. Poor Peter, Fran remembered, when he was little, used to complain that Granny had bristles on her chin and they prickled when she kissed him. The heavily pouched eyes, once the clear blue of Rodney's, had been washed pale by all the tears she had shed through the years. And poor Mama cried easily, sunk in self-pity. Today she was not quite as tearful as usual because she was on the warpath about the hotel. Any sort of quarrel revived her spirits.

She finished the list of grievances with a malicious attack upon a certain Lady Cotts in the hotel – a harmless-looking little woman whom she had pointed out to Fran during lunch. Mama said she had confided something or other to Lady Cotts who had repeated it to the manageress, and made mischief.

"I don't think I can possibly stay on here. Maybe you'd drive me round before tea and we'll look for another hotel. If not, I could try Brighton. I've been told about a very good hotel in Hove, no more expensive than this, and as you saw for yourself, the standard of food here is going down. Look how tough the meat was! I couldn't get my teeth through it."

"I ate all mine," said Fran cheerfully.

"Well, of course. Maybe it's because my new plate doesn't fit," admitted Mrs. Grifford.

Now, breathing wheezily, she folded her hands over her large stomach, while Fran set out to try and prove that by forsaking this hotel, Mama would be put to a lot of trouble and expense. She had so many of her own bits and pieces in her bedroom and the hotel in Hove might prove to be just as bad. She did at least like the manageress here and the air suited her. *And*, Fran reminded her, she used to say that she found Eastbourne more respectable than Brighton. Mama was dead-nuts on respectability. The mini-skirt, slacks, awful words like 'homosexuality', or the dreadful 'Pill', should not be mentioned.

"England is sinking, dear, sinking. I hardly like to read the newspapers. Even the best of them report such terrible cases these days."

Fran smiled and said in her most soothing voice:

"I know, but try and stick it out here for the rest of the autumn, Mama dear. Don't get all het up and move without thought. And don't worry about the sweets. Maybe the poor chamber-maid's mouth watered when she saw them and she couldn't resist."

Mrs. Grifford blinked through her glasses.

"Then she had no right to open my drawer and look," she said triumphantly.

Fran swallowed, and produced a parcel which so far she hadn't had time to give her mother-in-law. There'd been so much gossip.

"Here, dear, from your darling boy, with love."

Mrs. Grifford, on the verge of another onslaught upon the chamber-maid paused, and took the parcel. She adored getting presents. She could quite well afford to go out and buy as many sweets as she needed, but to be *given* them was so much better. She lifted the box of Charbonnel et Walker chocolates and clicked her plate.

"My favourites! Oh, how good!"

"Rod knows what you like."

"Don't you tell me that Roddy bought these. He gave you the money and *you* got them," Mrs. Grifford said with a cackle of laughter, popped a violet chocolate-cream into her big, red, smudgy mouth with relish, then hastily passed the box to her daughter-in-law.

Fran smiled. The old girl was really quite lovable in her way, tiresome though she was, and not unintelligent at odd times. She worshipped her only son and had spoiled him when he was a child. Her worship was responsible, in Fran's estimation, for so many of Rod's faults. The self-centred side; the enormous vanity; his refusal ever to see the other side unless it suited him to do so; and the strange spitefulness that rose up in him like gall when anybody tried to get the better of him.

All this, Fran felt sure, could be traced back to Mrs. Grifford's stupidity and the fact that she had protected and indulged her son in secret although his father who had been a sensible man had tried to discipline the boy.

Now, in her old age, Mrs. Grifford began to see her son's failings. When it came to speaking the truth she had to admit that Rod neglected her, whereas Fran was a loyal and devoted daughter-in-law. She never found fault with Fran. And she doted on her grandson, although she felt that it was a pity he was not tall, fair, and handsome like his father. He was his mother's boy. However, none the worse for that.

She wasn't satisfied until she had heard all the latest news about her little Peter. Not so little, Fran laughingly corrected the old lady. He was filling out, and had grown two inches. He seemed to be very happy at his new school.

"What sacrifices his grandfather and I made to send him there!" said Mrs. Grifford.

"I suppose you might say Rod and I made a few."

"Nobody these days sends their sons to Public School on income, my dear."

Mrs. Grifford, never tactful, could rarely get through an entire conversation with her daughter-in-law without mentioning Miranda.

"It was our poor little girl's birthday yesterday, wasn't it? I always remember it."

"Yes," said Fran, and her face froze.

Mrs. Grifford hastily changed the conversation. In her faintly malicious way – inherited by Rodney – she could not resist just the smallest desire to remind Fran that she should never have left the child alone even for those few fatal minutes. But immediately Mrs. Grifford said or did anything nasty she regretted it. It was just that she could not resist it when the opportunity came.

It was the signal for Fran to get up and announce her departure.

"Rod and I are dining out. It'll take me quite a time to get back to town, Granny."

"Give the dear boy my love and tell him to come down soon," was Mrs. Grifford's last remark.

Fran returned to London somewhat depressed.

Rodney came home late. When Fran, who was already bathed and dressed, reminded him that they were due at the

Locks' flat in half an hour, Rodney called out from his dressing-room:

"Too bad. I've only just started to shave. They'll have to put up with it. They will dine so damned early."

"Harriet Lock has a cook, dear, and you have to do what your cook wants these days, and hers likes to see some favourite T.V. series that comes on at eight-thirty."

"Cripes!" came Rodney's voice with a short laugh. "I couldn't do with modern staff. Harriet and Ted can let themselves be controlled by the kitchen if they want. Not me!"

No, thought Fran with amusement, *you let me do it all.*

She looked at herself in her dressing-table mirror, Rather a beautiful one that she and Rodney had picked up in an antique shop in Wales on their way back from a weekend at Portmeirion, rather a long time ago now.

In her consciousness there were two distinct phases of life with Rod. Pre- and post-Miranda. While Pete was still a baby they had left him with Nanny and gone to Portmeirion. Fran used to look forward to these occasional jaunts with Rodney as a kind of second, third, or fourth honeymoon. They had seemed so divinely happy in those days. But now the shadow of their little lost daughter lay between them even after eight long years. Not that Rodney ever spoke of it. But he was not the same Rodney who had taken her to Portmeirion.

"You must be glad your devoted wife is also a dedicated cook," she called out, put the last touch of mascara on lashes which really did not need darkening. She decided that she looked very tired tonight and wished that they could have had an evening at home. But one thing she had learnt about Rodney was that he did not like quiet domestic evenings. He did not like television either – only certain sporting programmes. Peter was mad about pop music.

This was their fourth night out in succession. Tonight it would mean dinner and bridge with the Locks. Harriet and Ted were both good players. Rod was good too. Fran was the worst player of the four, which meant she would have to mind her p's and q's and not play as though she were tired or it would disappoint her husband. She could not stand the bridge post-mortems, although on the whole Rodney was never nasty when she played badly and let him down, but he went to great pains to tell her where she had gone wrong. Somehow, lengthy discussions about her calling or playing, no matter how nice Rod was, seemed to confuse and upset her. But she liked Harriet Lock. Ted had been at Cambridge with Rodney and was now a successful businessman in the advertising world. They had no children.

Fran had put on one of the dresses that Rod liked her in best – a short greeny blue satin, plain and well cut. Long gold earrings, and bracelet to match.

She looked very smart. She had kept her neat, petite figure and Rodney was never slow to praise her, but it rarely seemed to go further than the odd compliment. She had begun to be aware of the fact that he hadn't come into her bed for the last two or three months. Yes, it must be quite that.

They used to share a double divan in which she now slept alone. For a year he had used the bed in his dressing-room; on the grounds that he snored and it was more restful for her to be alone. She had made the awful mistake of telling him once about that snoring. She felt unhappily sure it was now being used as an excuse rather than a sincere reason for his not sharing her bed. But she was far too proud to beg him to return. That was something she would never do.

He was putting on his shoes while she gave him his mother's message.

"Thanks," he said, "and thanks for trekking down to see the old dear. How was she?"

Fran explained why she had gone to see Granny, and Rodney looked up with a grin. The sort of grin that made him look younger and which warmed her heart. Pete looked like his father when he smiled that way.

"Mama and her thieving chamber-maids. She oughtn't to stuff all those sweets herself, anyhow. She's too fat."

"She'd like to see you, Rod. You haven't been down to Eastbourne for a fortnight, you know."

"We'll go on Sunday."

"Darling, we're going away – to Poole."

"Oh, to the Wiltons." His face lit up. "So we are. We can't put that off."

No, thought Fran, he wouldn't. Joe Wilton was a millionaire and a valuable client at Rodney's firm. She rarely discussed business with him but she knew that Joe was very important – involved with huge Unit Trusts. And when things were difficult, Rod always said "thank God for Joe". Besides which, the Wiltons had a glorious house overlooking Poole Harbour and a glorious boat in which Rodney loved to sail. Joe's wife, Janie, was an American, smart and amusing, much younger than Joe. She adored organising big house-parties but it meant a lot of drinking and possibly playing poker until the early hours, and Fran didn't much care either for sailing, or drinking – or poker. She only did all three to please Rodney.

"Well, when will you go down and see your mother?" Fran asked.

"Oh, don't nag me about that now," he snapped. "Let me finish dressing or we really will be late."

She looked at him. She could never do so without some of the old ache in her heart. He was as good-looking as the day she had married him – tall and very little heavier and at thirty-eight there was only a little puffiness under the eyes. But he still looked wonderful – in his prime, really. And he had the sort of physique that was the pride and joy of his tailor. Well-cut suits looked so good on Rodney. She liked the dark-blue he had chosen this evening, with the faint stripe, and the crisp whiteness of his shirt and collar. He had fine, well-kept hands. She watched him for a moment in silence as he strapped on the gold wrist-watch that she had given him a couple of Christmases ago, then smoothed back the crisp gold of his hair. He was a very shining man, Rodney, she thought.

Suddenly an unconquerable wish to get close to him pushed her through the usual barrier which she put between her emotional feelings and good sense. Usually she feared a rebuff. She walked up to him, nuzzled her cheek against his shoulder and murmured:

"I must say, I do take kindly to my handsome husband."

He put his arm around her, and gave her a hug.

"You still flirt with me, you funny one."

"Is it funny?" she asked wistfully.

"Sweet," he said, lightly kissed her hair then pushed her away, looking at her out of the corners of his eyes. "Come on, darling, or we will be late," and added: "Now look what you've done."

What had she done? She looked. There was a smear of powder on his suit. She bit her lip and brushed the mark away.

"Sorry."

She could see that her apology had no more effect on him than her sudden show of tenderness. She wondered a little cynically why she had so far forgotten the long years as to try and coquette with her husband. He had never been the sort of man to respond to that sort of approach. After their marriage it hadn't taken her long to learn that Rodney was a practical, not a romantic man–absorbed in himself and his own interests. Love-making between husband and wife was for the bedroom, or for sudden moments of passion in lovely lonely places where they could turn to each other if mutually stirred. Such moments, of course, had grown fewer as time went by. Sometimes Fran wondered whether it was like that with all married couples. It always seemed to be the man who accepted – preferred, in fact – a more platonic day-to-day association, while the woman retained a secret hunger for her romantic lover of the honeymoon.

Yet Rod was unpredictable. There were moments when he could still draw her mentally and physically close, and charm her into her original state of blind happiness; give her a delicious sense of warmth which made her feel that the frustrations and disappointments – and even the occasional rejections – were worth it all.

Such a moment came tonight as they drove in a taxi to the Locks' flat in Fountain Court. Rodney didn't want to be bothered with parking his car, or putting it away at a later hour.

Suddenly he put an arm around her and kissed her cheek.

"You really are a sweet thing, Fran. I'm bloody awful to you at times and I know it – but I appreciate all you do for me and thanks for being so nice to Mama. She can be a frightful bore."

"Oh, I'm very fond of her," said Fran loyally, "and she loves every hair of your head, so don't forget it."

"I don't. I just get irritated . . ." He sniffed at her hair . . . "Nice scent, darling. What is it?"

In the dusk of the taxi her large brown eyes gleamed amusement at him.

"You ought to know. You chose it. You brought it back from Paris – don't you remember? It's Guerlain's *Shalimar*. You said you liked the rather musky tang."

"When I was in Paris —" he began and stopped.

His arm dropped away. Fran's big moment was over, but she was enormously cheered. She refreshed Rodney's memory, gaily.

"You went over to meet your famous French client, *Monsieur* Something-or-other, at the beginning of the month.'

"Oh, yes," said Rodney abruptly. "My memory's getting appalling."

"So's mine, darling. So's everybody's. They say it's something to do with the pace we all live at. Nobody remembers a *thing* unless they write it down."

"Here we are," he said, jumped out, and opened the door for her.

He's really very nice, she thought. He never really means to be horrid. Darling Rod! I know him so well. He's stopped thinking about my perfume. He's wondering now if he'll get some good cards and take someone's money tonight.

The thoughts of Rodney Grifford, as he followed his wife into Fountain Court, did in fact circle around his wife's perfume; but not in the way she might have imagined. He hadn't even bought the stuff. He was in Paris on the 1st September, true enough, and true he had had an interview with M. Henri de Lasseur. But the business lunch had not been the main object of the operation. He had spent that forty-eight hours in the French capital for quite another reason; and not for the first time.

It was his third, madly exciting and all too brief weekend with Perdita. Perdita, who for the last five months had been his mistress.

4

It was while Fran and young Peter were in Jersey, staying for a week with Fran's aunt who lived there that Rodney first met Perdita Shaw. It seemed to him that the whole of his life was encompassed within those tempestuous days.

Fran's Easter visit to Jersey was an annual event. Her aunt who was a spinster, adored Peter and was going to leave him her money. And it was always the same – Fran didn't want to leave Rodney alone but made the visit for her son's sake. Rodney, with an eye to the main chance, persuaded her that it was the right thing to do.

He had quite enjoyed his week of freedom in the past, spent mainly with his men friends; out to dinner, gambling and sometimes spending the odd hour or two in the company of some woman who mildly attracted him. But on this particular occasion, things were different.

He stayed at home the day Fran left because he was busy and he had a lot of letters to write. He missed her. She was a very devoted wife and he found the house empty without her. He was also touched by the reluctance with which she always left him, although he knew that she trusted him absolutely.

He was not a man of extreme conscience so it did not worry him that he had betrayed that trust, not once but twice during their marriage.

The first time had been after Miranda's death. God, how hard *that* had hit him! He had plunged into a brief affair with a widow named Louise Parflet who had for some time been in love with him. She was in her early forties and very charming. When removed from sexual desire, she had seemed to him rather a sensible creature who had been good for him. She had even told him in the end that she had no intention of continuing with their affair because she realised that he had made love to her only on the rebound from the tragedy of Miranda.

Apart from this, Rodney had no wish to hurt Fran. He was well aware that he had behaved like a bastard to her at a time when he should have been understanding and tolerant. When the affair with Louise ended he returned to Fran's arms with more tenderness than he had shown in the past.

After that, he had tried to settle down to being a good husband, and a useful father to Peter – but there was another woman while he was in Austria, on a ski-holiday with one of his old University friends. That, however, had been brief and not really as satisfactory as the affair with Louise. Once more he returned to Fran full of good resolutions.

But his restless moods persisted.

It was while Fran and Peter were in Jersey five months ago that he met Perdita. George Stirling, who was on the Stock Exchange with Rodney, persuaded him to join a party at the Mirabelle.

George, a bachelor, was a great gambler and played a lot of roulette in the various Casinos in England and France. Rodney enjoyed it in a desultory fashion. He liked George's company. He was amusing and seemed to have a genius for gathering together attractive female company at a moment's notice. This time he told Rodney they were going to look after a couple of youngsters. His twenty-one-year-old niece, Belinda, whom he had promised to take out, and her friend, called Perdita Shaw.

"Perdita!" Rodney had repeated with raised brows. "What a name."

"Hope she won't be a bore, old boy, I haven't met her but Belinda say's she's just left Oxford with an Honours degree in Natural Science."

"My dear old George, I'm sure I won't be any good with a blue stocking," Rodney had protested.

But George argued that his niece had assured him that Perdita was as good-looking as she was clever. So Rodney eventually met them at the Mirabelle where they were to dine. And if he knew George, it would mean probably going on to Crockfords afterwards, perhaps when the two 'old men' had sent 'the children' home to bed.

The first sight of Belinda's friend came almost as a shock. Blue stocking be blowed; and she must undoubtedly be very clever to get a First in a subject like Natural Science, but he found it extraordinary that she should possess that sort of brain. She should have been a model, he decided. She was breathtakingly beautiful. Exceptionally tall. She made George's niece Belinda look tiny, although she was not really a small girl. She also made Belinda look insignificant and colourless.

Fran was small, and Rodney just on six foot in his socks, was used to looking down at her. Once he had a penchant for small fragile women. Perdita Shaw's eyes almost levelled with his. She was thin and willowy but had rather square shoulders and exceptionally long legs and hands. She gave an impression of strength and an almost Nordic beauty, although he learned that she was purely English. The brains were obviously handed down from her father, who was a well-known scientist in his day. Neither of her parents was living.

It had come almost as a shock to Rodney to look straight into those cool blue eyes – as blue as his own. She was very fair and wore her hair, which was straight and golden, in one big curve away from her forehead, falling down to her shoulders. Women as a rule did not look at him quite so coldly. Her long fingers barely touched his when they shook hands.

It was only after he had been watching her for a moment or two that he was conscious of further shock. She reminded him of someone he knew. Then his thoughts went further back. *Of someone he had known.* Miranda. Of course! His little daughter had had those same large light blue eyes, with lashes that were tipped with gold. And that delicate pale skin, those delicately cut lips.

There could be no real resemblance between a two-year-old child and a young woman of Perdita's age. He recognised the fact that it was a sheer flight of fancy, but the likeness was enough to endear Perdita to him immediately.

Her rather spectacular looks were enhanced by the Spartan simplicity of a short black dress which showed her knees. She wore no jewellery.

The next thing he noticed when they sat at the bar drinking before they took their table, was how little she drank. No gin. Only a Dubonnet with ice. He was to grow used to ordering Perdita's Dubonnet and ice.

"You seem to surround yourself as well as your drinks with ice," he teased her that night.

"Ice is only dangerous when it is hidden," she raised her glass and tinkled the little cubes. "This one makes music."

Well, he thought, iceberg she might be, but she, also, made music – extraordinary harmonies with an impact that both stunned and fascinated him. As far as he could remember he had never before been so interested in a girl of her age.

In one way she seemed untouched yet not at all immature. Very much a woman for her twenty-two years. Cool, poised, self-possessed. In the past he had avoided clever girls, but this one drew him like a magnet. There were times during the evening when he really failed to understand what she was talking about, and he gathered that she was working but attending special lectures at night and hoped to get a job eventually as a Computer Analyst.

There were other times when he felt a greater understanding as he watched her pale pink glistening lips widen into a smile which gave sudden warmth to her otherwise serious, rather bony young face.

He wanted to take her to a night-club when they left the Mirabelle, but she refused. George's niece was willing to prolong the evening's entertainment but Perdita said she must go home.

Rodney protested.

"Surely you're not so wedded to work that you can't enjoy a little relaxation?"

She turned those large turquoise eyes on him and smiled.

"I enjoy my work just as much as my fun," she said, then delighted him by criticising her own remark:

"Oh lord, how smug! I really mustn't say things like that."

She was not, however, to be persuaded to go on to the night-club with him. So, feeling rather bored, Rodney ended the evening by gambling with George. The one bright spot was that George's niece had told him when they said good-night that her friend Perdita thought him, Rodney Grifford, attractive.

The next morning George met him at lunch – they nearly always shared the same table – and Rodney tried to find out more about Perdita, but George knew little if as much as Rodney.

"Don't you think she's fantastic?" Rodney asked.

"Too tall for me. I like 'em petite," was George's laughing reply.

"Well, I found her most intriguing," said Rodney.

"Now, now, you're a married man, and Fran's a poppet," George grinned at him.

"Of course," Rodney agreed.

But the fact that Fran was 'a poppet' could not stop him from thinking a great deal about the tall blonde girl with her ice-cold brain. Last night he had wondered whether Miranda would have looked like that if fate had allowed her to live.

During the morning he 'phoned Perdita. He knew her number. He had taken pains to find it out; also that she was sharing a flat in Chelsea with two other girls.

"I'm a grass-widower," he had told her, "take pity on me and come to a theatre or something tonight. I'll get seats for anything you care to see."

He was nettled when she refused. She had already got a date, she said.

Fran and Peter were returning home at the end of the week. He only had this one week of freedom, and he experienced a strangely insistent desire to see this girl again.

"Can't you break your date and come out with me, Perdita?" he asked.

"I never break dates," was her answer. She had a quick, decisive way of speaking.

He persisted.

She told him briefly that she did not want to alter her plans. She was going to a lecture given by a visiting professor on Computer Analysis.

Rodney groaned.

"How can anybody as beautiful as you be interested in such subjects?"

"You've no idea how attractive I find them," was her laughing reply.

But she relented sufficiently to agree that he should fetch her from the hall where the lecture was taking place, and she would have some supper with him. She would be free at ten o'clock.

He met her with the car and drove her to a small attractive restaurant off the King's Road, recently opened, and offering specialities in shell-fish which, he was delighted to discover, Perdita enjoyed. Fran could never eat lobster or scampi. They upset her.

While he ate that meal with Perdita, he wondered whether this superb young thing – this five-foot-ten of golden youth – could ever suffer from such a mundane complaint as indigestion.

"You make me feel quite elderly," he laughed at her.

"How old are you?" Her cool blue eyes held, he thought, only faint curiosity. He wished he could rouse her to the sort of feminine interest he was accustomed to receiving from girls.

When he told Perdita his age, she only smiled and sipped her wine. She had a very long neck, he noticed, and she arched it backwards to swallow the last drop of wine. Rodney wished, also, that he had been a sculptor. He didn't know one, but he had a friend who was a superb amateur photographer. He must ask Paul to get a shot of Perdita Shaw drinking wine.

"Well, you've made no comment on my great age," he grinned at her.

"Nothing to say."

"I suppose you think I'm fishing and just want you to tell me that I look younger than thirty-eight?"

Even as he spoke, Rodney felt that he was being a bit naive – strangely so for him. He prided himself, as a rule, on being more subtle with women. It was curious that Perdita seemed to make him feel foolish. Then she gave him her delightful smile.

"Aren't you an egotist?"

That shocked him, too. Of course he knew it. He had heard it before from Fran, and took it from her. But he did not like to be criticised adversely by women he hardly knew.

"Aren't all men egotistical?" He signalled to a waiter to give Perdita more wine.

"I'll ask a computer when next I get a chance," she said.

"You and your computers! You're so very unlike the kind of person I imagine deals with punched-cards and electronics and so on. It amazes me."

"I adore electronics," she said.

"Do you only like things mechanical? Is the poor egotistical human beneath your notice?"

"Not at all," she said, and spoke gravely, as though it were a serious problem, "I like the company of men. I like my girl-friends, too, but men are better companions in a way. Even your best girl-friend is apt to get suddenly jealous or take offence too easily, or she tries to muscle in on your own love-affair."

Now Rodney's handsome face creased into humour. He sat back, jabbing a little silver cutter that Fran had given him, into the end of his cigar. Perdita had already announced that she did not smoke. He wondered what she *did* do apart from her work. But at least she had allowed the word 'love' to enter her vocabulary. He felt encouraged.

"So you do prefer the company of men?"

"Yes, and if you'd like me to say so, I'll admit that I rather like going out with you, Rodney."

This was unexpected. His pulses reacted to her sudden interest in him personally.

"I can't think why you like it but if I say that, I suppose

you'll accuse me of fishing again, so I'll just ask you why, as I obviously must appear to you as a kind of uncle or father-figure with a preference for earthly pleasures – I *am* a Philistine, you know."

"Oh, I have my moments," said Perdita. "I'm not at all like a machine, and unlike the best computer, I make mistakes."

"I've been told they do, too."

"That's what we're trying to eliminate. It should be impossible for a computer to be wrong."

"All the same, I can't take to the idea of a human being who is perpetually right. For me it conjures up the picture of an – er —" He broke off, shrugging. "I don't know how to put it into words."

"A smug perfectionist."

Rodney leaned across the table, cigar suspended between his fingers.

"Promise me you'll never become like that."

She laughed.

"You do amuse me."

"And you baffle me."

"I bore you, I'm sure. Men like girls to be flirtatious and ready to drop into their arms."

"I'm well aware you'd never drop into any man's arms."

"Oh, I did once," she said casually.

"You mean when you were a small child some fellow lifted you up and you stayed there."

"I don't mean that at all. When I was at Oxford my first year, I fell for one of the dons."

"Didn't you like boys of your own age?"

"Not much. They practise on you. I'm nobody's piano."

"You prefer the hand that plays the perfect tune straight off?"

"If you like."

That consoled him. At least he had established that Perdita didn't like very young men. Then he heard about her don whom she did not name but described as being a year older than himself, shorter than *herself*, balding, with strong glasses, and, she said, one of the most wonderful brains in the world.

"So you fell in love with a brain?" Rodney said.

"I don't suppose it was really falling in love. He just fascinated me. I slept with him twice. It was wonderful."

Her blue eyes glowed with memory.

Rodney blinked at his cigar. Extraordinary girl! Typical of the modern generation. Quite unmoved while she announced that she had lost her virginity and that she had enjoyed it. He could not somehow associate her sex-life with a short, bald, bespectacled professor. He felt almost a sense of indignation. And of course it was during that particular evening that he vowed to make this gorgeous, difficult, and quite astonishing girl experience the sort of love that he could show her. He had been told by the other women in his life that he was a first-rate lover. He was determined that Perdita should think so, too.

When later he left her at her flat he did not try to kiss her. He was going to show her that he also could play the hard-to-get game, and he was sensitive enough about women to realise that Perdita would neither fall for nor appreciate an effort to sweep her off her feet. She just wasn't to be swept.

But he asked her if she would meet him again.

"Or do I show too lamentable an ignorance of all the things you cherish?" he added.

The tall golden girl barely had to raise her eyes to answer the challenge in his. But he fancied, rightly or wrongly, that he saw something of warmth in them.

"I'd love to meet you again, Rodney. I think you're most —"

"Now don't say amusing," he interrupted.

"Don't you like to amuse your friends?"

"Darling, I've never fancied myself in the role of clown," he said lightly.

She put her head on one side and fixed him with a meditative stare.

"Now what rôle would you play well? Physically, you're the athletic type. I'm sure you play games well. But you're a bit smooth. Rather unusually so for the sporting type."

"You make me sound most unattractive."

"Oh, I assure you I used to be full of admiration for the

'Blues' when I was at University. I'm a strong healthy person myself and I like strong healthy men."

"Then a man in order to attract Perdita doesn't have to have a big brain in an undersized body?"

Perdita shook a falling strand of fair gleaming hair back from her face.

"That's malicious. I can see you dislike my don."

Rodney scowled. He couldn't do right with this girl and he knew it. He said:

"There's a lot of malice in you, too, you gorgeous creature. Anyhow, I was not only referring to your don. I was just saying that I'm glad you don't abhor the athletic type, if that is what I am. I only hope you like my smooth side. You see, I want you to like *me* . . . quite frankly."

"I don't often go out with married men," she said in her cool, level voice.

"Why not?"

"Oh, they say a lot of stereotype things about their unhappy lives and the poor wives who don't understand them."

"My life is quite happy on the whole," said Rodney stiffly, "and my wife understands me."

"Well, I'm glad," said Perdita.

"Then can we be friends?"

"I hope so. As a matter of fact I think you're . . ."

"Most amusing," he finished for her, glowering.

"You really are." She laughed and shook back the heavy mane of hair again. "Actually, it's great fun being with you. You're smart and rather good at repartee."

He took heart.

"I'm good at a lot of things, Perdita."

She stared at him in her cool, emotionless way.

"I'm sure you are. Tennis? Squash? Ski-ing? The stock market? Accounts?

"All correct. I'm said to be rather a genius with finance."

"How horrid!"

"No more horrid than one of your computers."

"Just that you don't expect them to be understanding. You feed knowledge into them, but they can't *feel*."

He stared at her.

"But my dear girl, I thought you were the type to shy away from feeling and that the punched-card system appealed to you."

"There are two sides to everybody, Rodney. My side that got me a degree in Natural Science is quite removed from the other side which accepts the existence of compassion versus cruelty or love versus hate. Living or dying, etc. – one could go on *ad-lib*."

"You're quite fantastic," he said, "and even though I may not understand half you say, I do in my way appreciate it, and I have a vast admiration for your mentality."

"Oh, I'm not original. Heaps of girls are machine-minded these days."

"I'm quite sure they're not like you."

"You're very nice," she said unexpectedly. "A wonderful host, and thank you for a marvellous supper. Incidentally, maybe some time or other I shall meet your wife."

The stars vanished from Rodney's sky.

"No doubt," he said, and cleared his throat. "Fran would be full of admiration for you. She's never passed an exam in her life but she thinks all you young girls of today who get the degrees and haunt the laboratories are splendid."

Perdita said:

"When I rang George to thank him for our party last night he told me that your wife was charming and that you have a small son, his godson, actually."

"Correct. Does that prevent us – you and me – from being friends?"

Perdita looked down at her feet, reflectively.

"No," she said.

He went home in a state of elation that he had not known for years and with a sense of mental and physical confusion into which Perdita had definitely plunged him. She made him think as no other woman had done. As yet he could not say he understood her. He only knew that hers was an attraction not as easy to forget as the others, both before and after Fran, who had figured so lightly and fleetingly in Rodney's love life.

Even when he was at the office, the memory of the tall fair girl troubled him. He had nothing to hang on to except the fact that she had stated categorically that the existence of Fran and Peter did not exclude him from her personal world.

She seemed to be very much alone in the world. Her mother had died when she was a child, and the spinster-aunt whose home she had shared since her childhood had suddenly married and gone out to New Zealand.

Rodney received a letter from Fran that next day, full, as usual, of tenderness, and of news of her's and Peter's holiday with Aunt Chrissie and how they both missed him. Fran's letters were always rather uninspired, even schoolgirlish, but loving and, like herself, unable to disguise the fact that she loved him very much. She couldn't wait to get back, she wrote.

But she didn't make the mistake of assuming that he missed her just as badly.

> "*I'm sure you're taking advantage of your freedom, and having a whale of a time. I hope you are . . .*"

After he read this Rodney felt strangely guilty: not that there was anything to feel guilty about, except that his 'whale of a time' was concentrated in the tall slim body of an amazing girl who on her own admission was not innocent.

He scribbled an affectionate note to Fran. He was haunted by the knowledge that he only had about another five days of this freedom from her. He found himself unable to resist telephoning Perdita again and inviting her to another meal.

He had to call her three times before he found her in and by then he felt an impatience, that was not with her but with himself. He was a damned fool to run like this after such a young girl. He'd always rather despised men of his age who paid attention to teenagers, yet, compared to Fran, to whom he had been marrried for fourteen years, Perdita seemed as old as the hills; in knowledge; in character. She had an extraordinary grasp of things, presumably part and parcel of that finely balanced brain of hers. An evening's conversation with her had proved that she was a poised young woman. When, finally, she spoke to him on the 'phone he was bitterly disappointed because she turned down his invitation. She was going out with one of her girl-friends, she said.

"And as you've told me before, you never break dates," he said rather acidly.

"That's right."

"Another lecture?"

"No," she laughed, "I'm not really like that, Rodney. We're going to a concert."

"So you prefer real music, to pop."

"Oh, I quite enjoy pop at times, but on the whole I prefer classical stuff. We're going to hear some Beethoven."

He was surprised to hear how pleased he was that at last he had found they had something in common.

"I'm sorry I can't come with you," he said.

"You'd be bored."

"On the contrary, I love Beethoven," he said triumphantly.

"Do you really?" She sounded surprised and slightly dubious, but he didn't let her go until he had proved that he was not just boasting. His father, he said, used to play an organ in their country house and was almost professional in his knowledge of both Bach and Beethoven. Rodney wasn't all that keen on Bach but he liked Beethoven and had one of the best collections of symphony records among his musical friends.

"If you'd like to come and hear them —" he began but altered it to: "or if it would interest you, and if you have a record-player, I'll bring a selection round to play to you. I think I've got the finest recording of the Ninth ever done, with Klempner conducting."

This seemed to surprise Perdita who answered with new respect.

"How thrilling! I always think the Emperor is the most wonderful of them all."

"My favourite is the Eroica," said Rodney.

That started them off on a lively discussion about the great composer's Symphonies, at the end of which Perdita said that she would be alone in the flat that next evening because her friends were going out. She had meant to do some sewing but she'd put it off, and he could bring round the records and she might even dare to give him a little food.

"No," said Rodney, "I'll take you out. We'll go and eat lobster at Gallanti's again, either before or after our session."

"No, I'll cook you a paella at home. I've been mad about Spanish food ever since I went to Madrid."

Rodney was not keen but answered with enthusiasm.

He wondered who took her to Spain but did not question her. It seemed a long time to wait till the next evening, but he felt content.

Fran respected his enjoyment of classical music, but her personal taste lay with light opera. She was a Puccini enthusiast and adored *Tosca* and *La Boheme* which he thought too sentimental.

It was splendid to have established a mutual love of Beethoven with Perdita. He was ridiculously pleased about it.

And that was how it all began.

5

THE Beethoven evening was a huge success, spoiled only by the fact that Perdita was no cook. Rodney found her paella almost uneatable and more suitable, he felt, for the young and hungry than for a man of his age. However, he swallowed the stodgy mess manfully and complimented her. When she asked if his wife cooked, he answered sincerely that Fran was Cordon-Bleu trained, whereupon Perdita gave him her icy blue stare and told him that he was lucky.

She had at least chosen a good white wine. They drank it most of the evening while they listened to the discs Rodney had brought.

Perdita seemed to enjoy them and he had never liked them more than when sitting like this, opposite her, watching her reactions to the music. The way her pencilled brows drew together and her heavy eyelids shut every now and again when a particularly stirring passage moved her. The way she marked time with her long slender fingers on the arm of her chair. The way she opened eyes that gleamed, full of enthusiasm.

This evening with Perdita was bliss for Rodney, even though he surreptitiously sucked a tablet for indigestion after eating all that heavy wet rice, tough chicken and prawns, dished up by his goddess. But, why, he asked himself with humour, should she be as good with cookery as she was with other things? To him she was touched by the gilt wings of some rare divinity. For the first time he recognised himself as a masochist because all too frequently she was unflattering in her criticism of him, yet he humbly accepted it.

After the music session ended they launched into a long philosophical discussion. She derided many of his personal views and he found himself painfully at a loss for words. So, while his eyes were filled with her beauty – she looked taller than ever tonight in black and gold slacks with a tight gold pullover showing the beautiful outline of her breasts – he cared not at all that he was unable to reach her mental level.

Whatever they discussed he found it necessary to tread warily so as not to make a fool of himself. A new experience for Rodney Grifford.

It was two o'clock in the morning before he left the flat. The friends who shared it with her were still away. He could have stayed longer. But it never entered his head to do so, or imagine Perdita had arranged this evening for any other reason than a friendly one. She had given no indication whatsoever that she expected him to make love to her. That was the intriguing, maddening thing about her, and had she not told him frankly about her love-affair with the Oxford don he would not have thought her much interested in sex.

She baffled and enthralled him.

During the week that followed he happened to run into a stockbroker acquaintance who had come across Perdita at Oxford.

"Diabolically brainy," he called her. He found her physically stirring, he said, but decided that he could not cope with any girl as clever – or as cool.

That was exactly how Rodney reacted, but he privately took the vow that he would 'cope' with Perdita, somehow or other, or perish in the attempt.

The week that Fran was away slipped by.

Rodney made no effort to play his habitual game of 'storming the citadel'. That might work with the average woman, but not, he was sure, with Perdita. He learned to be patient – to taken an altogether new line. He tried humility, and expressed a wish to learn rather than teach. This seemed to please her.

When he told her that he had never actually watched a computer work, she offered to take him down to the City to the offices where she held her temporary job, and where there were some of the most modern machines in the world. An American friend of hers was one of the directors. She arranged it all for Rodney. This man – Buster, she called him – was to meet them there and give Rodney a demonstration.

Rodney found the computers fascinating. The American seemed a nice fellow and was obviously one of Perdita's 'chums'. Perdita did most of the lecturing; Rodney watched and listened, fascinated by her grasp of the intricate machine. He told her, later, that he was beginning to understand her attitude toward modern science.

"I'll send you one or two books on it. You must study it," she said.

He told her quickly not to send them. He would pick them up. He could not imagine what Fran would think if she found a pile of scientific works in the house when she returned.

He felt stupidly annoyed when Buster kissed Perdita goodnight on parting. True, it was only on both cheeks. But they seemed to be on very friendly terms. Rodney was actually relieved when Perdita on her own account informed him that Buster was living with a French girl. She, Perdita, and the American had just become good friends after they had met at a party, and Buster had got her the job.

"I don't really like American men," she told Rodney. "They're sweet but they're such schoolboys. First of all, they make a girl feel rather soft and maternal, then they try to get her into bed."

"Is that what Buster did to you?"

She laughed and told Rodney not to be inquisitive. He spent the rest of the evening wondering whether Buster had been successful.

The week ended on a note of extreme frustration for Rodney, but he did not make the mistake of showing his feelings and letting his now definite passion for Perdita out into the open. They seemed to get on well – better every time they met. He was further cheered when his friend, George, playing chemmy with him at Crockfords one night, told him that he had found out from his niece that Perdita Shaw was 'rather keen' on him.

"I would never have used the word keen," Rodney replied with a short laugh. "I don't think Perdita is keen on any man. She's in love with machines and Beethoven. But we are just good friends."

"Cripes!" said George. "You sound like a film star landing at Heathrow with his mistress – making an announcement to the reporters."

Rodney was annoyed.

"Perdita is certainly not my mistress."

George clapped him on the shoulder and went off, guffawing, leaving Rodney to think he didn't really like Peter's godfather as much as he used to do. George was a bit of a fool. But the picture of Perdita as his mistress troubled Rodney's working hours and his nights. He began to sleep badly, which he had never done in the past.

Two days before his wife and son came home, he telephoned Perdita. She was booked for dinner and would not cancel the appointment even though he pleaded. He felt dejected and a little angry. He had refused a party which ordinarily he would have found amusing – only because he had anticipated that Perdita would meet him. Trying not to appear too disappointed he issued a casual invitation to her to take a drive in the Mercedes after her dinner-party. It was fine weather – she might like the air and then he would drive her home, he said.

She hesitated a second, then agreed to this.

"Okay – pick me up at the Savoy – side entrance – about ten o'clock."

It seemed to Rodney a long evening until ten o'clock. He was disgusted with himself for behaving and feeling like a love-sick boy. He was content only when he saw the tall fair girl and had seated her safely in the car beside him. She seemed in good humour and stretched her long legs luxuriously as he drove away, and along the Embankment.

"M'm . . . gorgeous car. My rich friend!" she murmured.

He gave her a sidelong glance.

"The present government, my sweet, doesn't allow men to be rich."

"Do you think England is going right downhill?"

"No. We'll never go right down – there's something in the English that won't allow that."

"The true Britisher waving his flag," she teased.

"Don't you wave one too?"

"Yes, but I'm unpatriotic enough to want to follow the queue of the brain-drain. Buster's firm have promised me a job in New York and I rather want the money. It's terrific."

He glanced at her classic profile as they headed for the Tower of London.

She looked disturbingly attractive and her beauty, seen frequently as the lights from street lamps and passing cars lit up her face and form, was devastating to him. When he had asked her where she wanted to go, she had said anywhere. He went on driving along the side of the river. It might be their last evening. The thought stabbed him until he could scarcely bear it. He was determined somehow to prevent a complete break with this fascinating girl.

"I thought you told me the other evening that you didn't particularly mind about money?" he reminded her.

"I don't in a way."

"Then why leave your own country in order to earn all those dollars in America?"

"Because it's difficult to save here and I want to make enough in order to take me a trip round the world. I don't mind roughing it but I need enough to get me places. I want to see every capital. I can work and study as I go, and find out what is being achieved outside Great Britain. I shall certainly go to Russia. I don't suppose you understand that? I suppose you think I ought to want just marriage with a nice healthy husband and a lot of children, and a settled home."

They had almost reached the now locked and guarded precincts of the Tower. Rodney pulled up and switched off the engine. It was a cold night of stars and frost. Perdita wore only a thin white wool dress and jacket but she didn't seem to feel the cold. He felt as he always did when he was with her, the warmth that glowed behind her frigid exterior. Rather gloomily, he said:

"No, I can't see you settling down in the domestic sense, and I am quite sure you could take care of yourself admirably travelling *toute seule* round the globe. I can even visualise you as the first British woman to enter a capsule, fly to the moon and land a computer there. You're an odd moon-like creature."

The corners of her eyes narrowed into laughter.

"Dear old Rodney! You say such . . ."

"Amusing things," he finished for her, then they both laughed. "But don't go away too far," he begged. "You'd be lost to me. I'd never see you again."

This with any other of Rodney's girl-friends would have been the signal for her to move nearer him and beg him not to go too far from her, either. But the unpredictable Perdita said:

"Oh, you'd survive!"

Rodney suddenly lost his head, which he hadn't done since he became Louise Parflet's lover.

"Damn you," he said thickly, pulled Perdita close to him and kissed her on the lips. For a moment she did not stir. She kissed him back but her lips were cool, without passion.

Then she drew back and laughed. It was the sort of tolerant, amused laugh that would have dampened any man's ardour. It put Rodney's passions straight to sleep. It was so amazing to him that she should behave this way – reversing their ages – she, like a mature woman, being tolerant with him, a young boy. It was quite fantastic how she managed to drag him down from the pedestal on which hitherto he had placed himself as an experienced lover to be reckoned with.

"That was very nice," she said. "Thanks, Rodney."

He gasped. A street lamp shone in her brilliant blue eyes. He could see the absolute futility of trying to make love to this girl. She was incapable of coquetry and, so it would seem, of ordinary desire. Or was it just that she didn't like *him*? How could she sit there, coolly thanking him for that kiss, whatever she felt, knowing how deeply it had disturbed him?

"Oh God," he muttered, "you do have a genius for putting a man in his place. I need a cigarette."

"Okay," she said and he saw her take a mirror and with the well-worn stump of a pink lipstick, outline the curve of that unresponsive mouth.

"I've thoroughly enjoyed this evening," she added brightly.

He believed that she meant it. She wasn't annoyed because he had kissed her. It just didn't matter.

Louise Parflet had been a sensual woman – he used to be able to light the fires in her with a single caress. Fran cuddled up to him like a warm affectionate kitten, wanting to be caressed.

He decided not to be so old-fashioned as to apologise for kissing Perdita. He put the cigarette between his lips and switched on the Mercedes.

"Better take you home."

She did not remind him that they had only just got together tonight.

She did little talking during the drive home and he remained sulkily silent.

"Thanks awfully for everything, Rodney, I adored your records the other night, too."

"How about coming out with me tomorrow?"

Crazy, of course, he told himself. He was dining with a client tomorrow, too. But money-minded though he was, he was even prepared to go sick and cancel the client if Perdita accepted.

Perdita astonished him by saying she was free, and adding that she would simply love to have another evening with him.

"I'll try and behave —" he began.

"Oh, Rodney, you do make me laugh!" she broke in.

He had never seen anything so beautiful, he thought, in a thoroughly frustrated way, as Perdita standing there in the moonlight.

He left her and drove home nettled yet delighted because she had agreed to meet him. She liked the Mercedes-Benz. She wanted to drive it. Tomorrow being Friday, she had said she could get away by five. He said, quite blatantly lying, that he would be free at the same time. He would drive out of London, then let her take over on the open road. They'd go down to Gatwick Manor Inn where they could have an excellent meal. She liked the idea of that. One of her girl-friends had been there lately and said it was great fun.

Rodney spent the rest of the night wondering how best to please Perdita.

6

WHEN Fran walked with her son into her house that Saturday, with Rodney following, carrying her case, she felt nothing but pleasure that she was home again.

Peter, looking browner and better for his week in Jersey, despite little sun, rushed upstairs to his room to examine his collection of chrysalises. He had every hope that they would turn into magnificent butterflies rather than insignificant moths, which his father had told him was the more likely.

Fran untied her head-scarf, threaded her fingers through her short dark hair and looked up at her husband with glowing eyes.

"It was sweet of you to meet us, darling."

"Why not?"

"Jersey seemed such a long way away although it's only just across the water."

"How was your Aunt Chrissie?"

"Fine, and she thinks Peter has put on weight and is growing into a charming boy. I must say he was awfully nice to her and he has a way with elderly women, has our Peter."

Rodney grunted. Then said what was expected of him.

"You're looking good, Fran. Enjoyed your week?"

"I was thoroughly spoilt. I wasn't allowed to get up to breakfast and Aunt Chrissie did all the cooking and she has a daily so I've been quite lazy – hardly allowed in the kitchen."

They were up in Fran's bedroom. Rodney walked to the window and looked out. It had been a grim drive back from Heathrow. It was pouring with rain. Just to the right he could see Eaton Terrace looking particularly grey and deserted. A grey day all round. Greyness in his mind, too. He felt remorse because he was not pleased that his wife and son had come back. Guilty because every pulse in his body was still beating for Perdita.

Last night . . .

Fran interrupted his thoughts.

"I expect you've missed us. There's nothing so empty as an empty house when everybody is away except you."

"Yes, of course," Rodney said perfunctorily, "it's been very – er – lonely."

Fran gave him her slow sweet smile, then walked to her dressing-table. It was a golden walnut spinet – one of her favourite pieces of furniture, and the best old Mrs. Grifford had given them.

This was a beautiful room, with two tall windows and a wrought-iron balcony. The curtains were old-gold, and the carpet grey. The bedspread on the big double divan a glorious lime-green velvet with gold fringe. Fran had 'gone to town' over her bedroom. When they had moved here she had told Rodney she wanted a really luxurious room with a lot of dignity and beauty, and no frills.

He approved of the things she had chosen and one of his Christmas presents was the fine oil-painting by a French artist, hanging over the fireplace. Fran had fallen in love with the old Provençal house in the picture, and its shadowy background of mountains. The greens and golds toned with her décor.

Rodney used, of course, to come into this room so much more often than he did now, but it was still the room she liked best in the house. She had her little Queen Anne bureau in one corner and her own books, and she wrote her letters in here. The drawing-room somehow was more formal, and for entertaining, like the pine-panelled dining-room.

Now she bent and inhaled the perfume of the yellow hothouse roses on her table. They were still in slim folded beauty of bud on long green stems emerging from the cut-glass vase. She lifted the card beneath them and read:

"*Welcome home siempre.*
Rod."

For a moment she could not speak. Her sight was blurred by the sort of tears she so rarely let him see these days. He always had flowers waiting on her dressing-table after she had been away. He never forgot. One of Rodney's most endearing qualities was his generous tribute to her adoration for flowers and her sentimental liking for this sort of welcome. Lover, he might no longer be, but as a husband she really could not complain. Today there seemed nothing to complain about at all. He seemed in the best of humours and full of bright conversation on the way back from Heathrow. He had also been particularly chatty with Peter, and listened to the boy's stories about what he had done in Jersey.

She did so long to establish a real contact between those two.

Now she looked at Rodney and indicated the roses.

"You never forget. Thanks awfully, darling."

"Oh, not at all," he said rather awkwardly.

She went to him. The week away from him had seemed so long. She wished she did not care so much about her husband. She wished she could be like some of her friends, fond of their 'better-halves' but no longer very sentimental. Fran had learned to check her emotions but only up to a point, and now she was suddenly beyond that point. She put her arms around the tall handsome man and hugged him against her.

"Oh, darling Rod, it's good to be back."

"Darling," he said mechanically, and dropped a kiss on her hair.

She lifted her lips and closed her eyes.

Rodney looked down at that small fine-boned face and could do nothing else but embrace her. But when he touched her lips and felt the hunger in them, he drew back as though startled, and tried to bridge the perilous moment by a show of false gaiety. He kissed her twice rapidly, then said:

"Isn't it time I thought of something new to put on the card? I've almost forgotten how to spell *siempre*."

"I hope you haven't."

He knew he had said the wrong thing. They had spent their honeymoon in Spain where they had both picked up a little Spanish. After that he had always signed his letters to her with that which meant 'for ever'. And he *had* meant *for ever* when it all began. He had been very much in love with his small warm wife with her petite figure, her large brown eyes, and the charming way she used her hands and sometimes put her head a little to one side when she looked up to ask him a question.

It was damnable, he thought, that things had to change like this. Life was a trap. One went into one's marriage with absolute integrity and the genuine conviction that the passion would endure. Then one learned that it didn't. Custom and habit are the enemies of love. Passions cool. And when a man was nearing forty and had been married as long as he had, it seemed somehow necessary to find something new – in order to rouse him – something *different*.

He didn't want the thought of Perdita to steal into his mind at this moment. He had tried to pretend to himself that he wouldn't let last night make any difference. He didn't want to hurt Fran. Poor little thing – she loved him so much. And although he knew that the hideous memory of Miranda's death had through the years crept between them like a slow insidious poison, he had honestly forgiven her for that split second of carelessness and now at long last begun to see that it was worse for her than it had been for him, because she blamed herself. Anyhow, it was all so long ago. It wasn't because Miranda had died that he had fallen out of love with Fran. It was just one of those things.

When he had met Perdita and she had reminded him of his little dead daughter, she had somehow walked straight through whatever chinks there were in his armour, and it had never really been an impregnable one. He was often astonished to find how vulnerable he was.

"I'll never forget Spain – of course I won't," he said abruptly, then walked past Fran and shouted up the stairs:

"Pete —"

"Yes, Dad?"

"Come on down. Walk to the Square with me. I've run out of cigarettes."

"I got some on the 'plane for you, darling —" began Fran but did not press the subject as he did not seem to hear her, and anyhow she was delighted that he should bother to ask Peter to go out with him even on so paltry an errand.

She was not unhappy as she heard them laughing together down in the hall. She walked to her bed, turned back the cover, and placed her suitcase on it. She pulled out the long carton of duty-free cigarettes and a bottle of Remy-Martin brandy which she had brought for Rodney.

Then she stared at the two pillows on the bed, one of which she knew would not be used. It was so long since Rodney had slept with her. He didn't love her any more – at least not in the way she wanted to be loved. Odd how it went on hurting even though she had resigned herself to the inevitable. She did not think there was another woman. She doubted if he was any longer interested in sex – but liked just to flirt in a gay idle sort of way. He had said this, once or twice, and she was quite certain that his job and his other outside interests were of more importance to him than the love of women. At the same time, Fran had never yet been separated from him for a week or more without coming home and experiencing the old thrust of the dagger right through her heart.

Spain . . . *siempre* . . . roses. No doubt they meant that Rodney still cared in his way and she only drove him further from her when she tried to get too close. But it *did* hurt.

Fran put her face in her hands for a moment, then rubbed her eyes with her knuckles as she had so often seen Peter do. With grim determination she went into the bathroom to run a hot bath.

When Rodney came back with Peter she was in slacks and a polo-necked jersey which suited her. She went downstairs to look around her kitchen. In the refrigerator she noted there was all she needed. Her excellent daily, Mrs. Crow, had got in the usual milk, butter, eggs, and fats. Mrs. Crow could be relied upon. She had only stayed away once in two years, and that was when her husband had had a stroke. Since then she had become the bread-winner of her family and worked furiously, not only for Fran but also for an American woman who lived two doors down.

The larder showed that Rodney, too, had been busy. Thoughtful. Smoked salmon. A cold, cooked chicken. A salad. He wasn't going to let her do much work on her first night home. One of Rod's most endearing qualities was the way in which he considered her at times like this. He was a strange contradiction. Utter egotism coupled with sudden warm bursts of affectionate regard, but my goodness, her thoughts ran on, he had to be handled carefully. It didn't take much to irritate him.

When he came back with the cigarettes – he had had to walk further than he thought to get them – she asked him, jokingly:

"Seen all your girl-friends while I was away, darling?"

Fran was bringing out the bottles needed to make a salad dressing. Rodney looked at the small busy figure and was glad that she could not see the redness had mounted his forehead.

"I haven't got any girl-friends," he snapped.

Fran turned a smiling face.

"I was only pulling your leg."

He changed the subject.

"You took the camera with you, didn't you? Get any good colour-photos of Jersey?"

"Yes, I brought them home to be developed. Several nice

shots of Peter I think. I'm just going to make a cuppa. I'm dying for one."

Rodney lit a cigarette and walked out of the kitchen. He also walked out of the house and round the corner to the nearest call-box.

He dialled the number of Perdita's flat.

7

PERDITA did not answer. This flung Rodney into a nervous state.

He decided that he could hardly stand putting on an act as the loving husband and father for the entire evening. He took a walk through Sloane Square and down the King's Road. Even on Saturday it was full of young people. He never knew whether to be amused or irritated by what he saw these days in this Chelsea stronghold. It was against his upbringing, his education, his general outlook to approve of the new generation – the young men with their long curling hair, their side-burns, and what Rodney called 'fancy dress'. He had squashed his own small son completely on the subject of 'Group behaviour and clothes'. Yet he knew that their influence had penetrated even the public schools. He had to admit that it was a very powerful one. And the girls, with their brief skirts, some looking like children with theatrically painted lips and black-lashed eyes. They seemed happy, herded together, drinking outside cafés on the pavements, or strolling up and down the streets with their arms linked, stopping now and again to kiss and caress each other.

This was the new world. It rather annoyed Rodney as it made him think of himself, and he felt sure these youngsters would think him a 'has-been' – an old fossil.

Inevitably his thoughts were of Perdita. She, with her high-precision mind, her particular intellect, could not be classed as one of the 'flower children', young though she was. She seemed far above and beyond the Pop-Group worshippers. She was *different*. It was that essential difference, her unique personality that had so completely enslaved Rodney. He would never have dreamed of betraying Fran with one of these girls strolling along the King's Road this afternoon. He hadn't meant to betray Fran at all. But Perdita had defeated him. She, who had never made a single effort to do so.

He remembered last night and was shocked that he could feel such a burning desire for her – for any woman. It was an almost unbearable longing, all the more so because the physical urge was no more fierce than that other madness. The madness of the mind. She had made, unconsciously perhaps, piecemeal of his feelings. Brought emotions into focus that he never dreamed he possessed.

He was no longer the same man, content with an average domestic life coupled with golf, sailing, his work on the Stock Exchange, his lunches with clients or business friends – and all else that had gone to make up the world of Rodney Grifford until Perdita entered it.

When he walked home through the dawn this morning he had realised that his whole outlook on life had altered. She had shattered his former belief that one attractive woman in bed was as good as another, and that a woman had a place in a man's life but must wait outside it until he desired her again.

When he had left Perdita, he STILL wanted her, madly, and wondered how he could carry on with his former existence – the one that did not include her.

Of course, neither of them had meant it to happen. When Perdita agreed to spend that last evening of his freedom with him before Fran's return, he had anticipated a recherché dinner somewhere or a film or even a concert if she preferred it, and a meal afterwards. Then goodbye.

Over the telephone they had arranged to meet at her flat. Once again, he made the interesting discovery that her two girl-friends were still away on holiday. One, Jacqueline Hurst, was a model. The other, Annabel Kaye, who was rather more of a friend to Perdita, was studying Biology at London University.

Perdita was not dressed when he arrived. As she opened the door, he was faintly amused to see that she looked taller than ever in a long white towelling dressing-gown. Yet she wore it as all her clothes – superbly. She was tying the sash around her long slim waist as he walked into the hall.

"Terribly sorry," she said, "I'm never very punctual."

He put his Burberry and scarf on a chair and smiled.

"Never?"

"So they say," she shrugged. "I lose count of time."

"I think I'd lose count of time if I saw much of you, my child," he said, and walked into her sitting-room and smoothed his hair back with both his hands.

"Really, Rodney, I do hate idle flattery."

He turned and looked at her. He had never seen her before with such a sulky droop to her lips. Lips that were a very pale pink. There was no make-up on her face. Neither was her hair brushed. But it still shone like silk, and she looked extraordinarily youthful in that wrapper. Her skin was fresh and unpowdered as though she had just stepped out of a bath. Not for the first time since he had known her, he compared her with his dead child.

"Are you going to be argumentative with me tonight?" he asked her, pulling a packet of cigarettes from his pocket and handing it to her with a smile. She shook her head.

"I expect I will," she said in her casual way.

"Then we ought to have a wonderful evening."

She gave that little shrug which he now recognised as characteristic, pursing her lips as she did so.

"Oh, I know you don't like arguing as much as I do."

"I do too, only I find it unattractive when it becomes acrimonious."

"Two intelligent people arguing should never become personal or acrimonious."

Now he laughed outright, clicked on his lighter, lit his cigarette and blew a cloud of smoke away from her.

"'Fraid there is only one intelligent person in any debate

you and I may have, my dear, and I'm not fishing! I know my limitations. I'm a fairly well-educated chap, a damned good mathematician, and a successful broker, but I can't pretend to reach your heights."

"I'm not as clever as you keep telling me," she said, and thrust her long thin hands into the pockets of her bath-robe. She seemed in no hurry to get dressed, but this was typical of Perdita who, once she became involved in a discussion, couldn't bear to let it go, no matter what else she ought to be doing.

"I know my limitations, too," she went on, "and because I've got a degree and have what I suppose you think a scholarly mind, I assure you I'm a novice when it comes to the really big brains. I'm always wanting to learn more."

"Since I've met you, I've wanted to learn more too, Perdita."

"About what?" she demanded, and fixed him with those blue strange eyes that always, somehow, took him off his guard. He replied lamely:

"All the things that interest you."

"I wouldn't have said so. You're too self-satisfied. I'm sure you have no particular desire to start learning anything."

Dammit, he thought. She certainly never flattered *him*. At times she made him feel almost a fool. If Fran had been half as critical or cruel he would have had a flaming row with her, then walked out. He was not accustomed to harsh criticism. Yet he took it from this young girl meekly, and came back for more.

"You're not always right, Perdita," he said, "and I'm not as smug as you think me. But one thing my association with you has definitely taught me – I'm a time-waster. Oh, I don't mean at my job – I'm a busy man and very successful, but I can see now I have not given enough time to more worthwhile things."

"Such as —?"

Rodney's brows creased. She would pin him down. He never had a ready answer to satisfy her. He knew she had no use for witty cracks, or any type of remark that she would label meaningless.

He decided to be honest, for this Perdita was above all things.

"I just don't know," he answered her, "but you make me think and I haven't given enough time in my life to deep thinking."

"Don't you and your wife have discussions?"

"Not the sort you like."

"You mean you either fight, like most married couples, or don't talk at all?"

Now his face reddened. Perdita was far too perceptive and often too near the truth.

He had a latent desire to be loyal to Fran, but he had to be truthful, so he explained to Perdita that Fran was just a sweet kind affectionate sort of woman who was engrossed in her life as a wife and a mother; that they led a busy social life, so there were few opportunities for getting down to discussions on the basic facts of life or living, and certainly didn't embark on philosophy or science.

Perdita went to a cupboard and pulled out two glasses and a bottle of sherry.

"Sounds awfully dull to me," she said.

He remained silent. She made it sound dull to him, too. Perdita had a dangerous facility for making a man want to jump out of his own skin and get into another. Into one not at all like Rodney Grifford. Suddenly he made a rather abortive attempt to defend himself – and Fran.

"We're quite an ordinary couple. That's what all marriages are like, you know. Rather boring after a time."

"Are they?"

Perdita gave him her cool critical stare and her eyes looked bluer than anything he had ever seen. The unstudied grace of her arm's movement as she lifted the sherry bottle up to the light to see how much there was in it, shook him. He felt a little sweat break out on his forehead. He was afraid of the sudden tempest of feeling she roused in him. He said through his teeth:

"Yes, they are, no matter how close a couple might be – no matter how fond of each other, after fourteen years which is how long Fran and I have been married – the average couple settles down to an ordinary sort of existence where things revolve around the home and the family, plus work and amusements and holidays and all the rest of it. Fran and I don't see eye to eye over a lot of things but how many husbands and wives do? Or are still so interested in what they have to say to each other that they spend hours talking like students or philosophers? I don't know any," he finished rather crossly.

"You must have a deadly lot of friends," said Perdita, and poured out a glass of sherry and handed it to him.

He took it and was not surprised to see that his hand was shaking.

"Look here, you aggravating child, if this is how you feel, why don't you find *me* deadly? I belong to the type you seem to despise. Why bother with me?"

She shrugged and seated herself on the arm of her dilapidated sofa. The flat was very shabby and quite unlike the sort of well-furnished and often beautiful homes which Rod and Fran visited. Yet between these four walls there existed for him a fascinating, pulsating atmosphere that he had never found anywhere else. An atmosphere that was *Perdita*. She seemed to dominate it and to make everything else around her become insignificant. She had begun to dominate him, which he found astonishing – and dangerous. He looked at her, sitting there with her legs crossed, fingering her glass of sherry. The dressing-gown had fallen away a little and showed the unusually long legs almost to the thigh. Her skin was like marble, white and smooth, without blemish, except for a faint golden down which he found most attractive.

"You haven't answered my question," he said.

"I was considering it."

"Well?"

She looked him straight in the eyes, the faintest upward curve to her lips.

"Poor Rodney – you do want me to say something nice, don't you?"

He put his own glass down on the table because his fingers were trembling now so that he could no longer hold the stem.

He felt an intense anger and frustration, mixed with his desire for her.

"Don't bother to come out with me," he said. "I'm sure you only accepted my invitation tonight because you knew I was alone and felt sorry for me. Surely you could have a more amusing evening with one of your own highly intellectual friends?"

Now she threw back that long column of throat and laughed, but not unkindly.

"Darling, you really are so immature, it isn't true. Are all stockbrokers the same? Perhaps most men are, and I'm still living in the student world. Up at Oxford we all talked and talked and talked and didn't care if we starved and there wasn't this atmosphere you describe of *invest your money properly. Get rich quickly. Buy expensive things. Send the children to Public Schools. Give the best dinner parties in town. Give the wife the best mink coat.* All that nonsense. I give you my word I'd never get married if that was the sort of life I'd have to lead. It would be too utterly defeating."

He crushed the end of a half-smoked cigarette on to an ash-tray.

Suddenly he wanted to be rude to her.

"I don't really mind whether you get married or not," he snapped. "And I don't like being treated as though I'm a fool."

She laughed again and held out her hands.

"Darling, you're no fool. But you're still a bit of a schoolboy, aren't you? So many Englishmen and Americans are. It's the way they're educated. But you've got tremendous charm, and, you're sweet and generous and you do rise when I tease you. You're so *easy* to tease. Don't be cross with me. I'm beastly. I'm sorry."

He relaxed. Her sudden use of the word 'darling' gave him some encouragement which increased when she stood up, came nearer him and said:

"Don't let's quarrel. Let's go out. I'll be good and promise to do exactly what you want."

He felt the blood mount to his forehead.

"Exactly?" He repeated the word significantly.

"Oh, really, you're the absolute end!" she laughed.

His resistance was by now a slender thread and it snapped.

"Don't you realise, you maddening girl, that I'm crazy about you," he said, and drew her into his arms. She did not move.

He laid one hand against her bare throat and felt the throb of the pulse there. He couldn't be sure and yet he would have sworn that this beautiful sculptured body had become pliant and warm, all of a sudden, and *human*. Galatea, come to life.

"God!" he said thickly, and kissed her squarely on the mouth.

It was not at all the same as the kiss they had exchanged in the Mercedes by the river that other night. Then, he had doubted that she was the least moved. Tonight was different.

She put her arms around his neck and moved closer to him. She said nothing, but her eyes closed. That was the instant of Rodney's triumph. When a woman wanted to be kissed, or was being kissed, she nearly always closed her eyes.

Perdita was all woman in his arms after that, and although still strangely silent for a girl who normally spoke with such rapidity and fluency on every known subject, her lips were eloquent. She seemed to enjoy the long kisses they exchanged, as much as he did. Her response filled him with an elation he had not experienced for long years. Neither with Louise, nor the girl in Austria, and never with Fran. (Poor sweet Fran!)

They did not go out that night. And Perdita did not dress.

He led her to the sofa. They lay there in each other's arms. It seemed to him, rightly or wrongly, that she was as hungry for his kisses and caresses as he was for hers.

He had known, of course, that she was not a virgin. For that, he was thankful. He had no great wish to seduce an innocent young girl – if there was such a thing still to be found in this day and age.

8

AFTER their passion was spent and by mutual consent, they sat together smoking, and sipping the wine that Perdita had cooled for him. She spoke about her first lover. Not that she used that old-fashioned term. It was extraordinary, Rodney thought, how elderly she was now making him feel at times. Even the don up at Oxford was just the boy-friend.

"Did you enjoy it with him as much as you did with me?" Rodney asked jealously.

Perdita looked at him with sleepy eyes and gave him an enigmatic smile.

"You shouldn't ask indiscreet questions."

Her throat and shoulders were still bare. He had just covered the rest of her magical body with her bath-gown. The thick golden hair tumbled to her white shoulders in a strangely wanton way that set him on fire. She had been marvellous and he told her so. But she wouldn't tell him that she thought him so, too. She only said:

"Well – I never meant that to happen."

He put down his cigarette, lifted one of her long hands and drew it across his lips.

"I don't care whether my question is indiscreet or not, I'd like to know if you enjoyed my love-making as much as *his*."

She evaded the question again.

"I knew somehow I'd like it, or I wouldn't have let it happen."

He took one of her fingers between his teeth and gently bit it.

"I've never met such a wretched girl! I positively dislike you."

She laughed outright.

"Then what do you do if you *like* a girl?"

He bent down and laid his hot cheek against hers. Still so cool to the touch, he wondered if that hour of intensely passionate love-making had ever taken place or if he had dreamed it.

"I'm terribly in love with you, Perdita," he said with genuine emotion.

Now she sat up, shook back her hair, and jabbed the end of her cigarette into the ashtray on the table beside her.

"It's not much good either of us being in love, Rodney. You're married and I'm dedicated to my work."

He was filled with a strange sense of defeat. Whatever move he made she seemed able to check-mate him. At the very moment when he imagined he had captured her wholly, she eluded him again. Perhaps that was her main attraction; but she both baffled and infuriated him even while he longed to experience that marvellous interlude of passion with her again.

He felt curiously depressed in this moment. He had never thought very profoundly about love and emotion, or men and women's reactions to each other. He did not imagine himself to be that sort of person. But he was sure now that he had met his Waterloo in Perdita Shaw.

It was going to be more than he could endure to walk out of this flat and out of her life just because he was married. The situation threatened to get out of hand.

When he remembered the other women in his life, he could see how different such affairs had been. He had always held the upper hand.

Louise, older than himself, had given him up voluntarily, and because she thought it best for him. But he had seen her once after their parting and felt sure he could have called her back at a word or a touch.

The girl in Austria had been difficult – one of those excitable, passionate women with Continental blood in her veins and a tendency to dramatise herself. He had soon found that it was no good trying to reason with *her*. He had got to be ruthless, slide out of the affair, return to England, *and* make sure he never saw her again.

And what of Fran? Her selflessness, her patient devotion? He reached the simple conclusion cynically, that he was not a nice character. He was too unstable. But these conclusions could not come between him and his profound desire for Perdita.

He told her so.

"I've never felt about any other girl in my life as I do about you. I'm married but it doesn't alter things. As for you being wedded to your work, all right now, but are you sure you'll never want to marry?"

Perdita blew a cloud of cigarette smoke into the air and locked her fingers behind her beautiful head. Her gaze met his with the usual cool honesty.

"I didn't say that. I know I will want to marry and have a family some day, but not for years. I didn't work like a nigger at Oxford and I'm not working like a nigger now, just for nothing. I'm mad about my work and I intend to carry on with it."

Rodney felt the sweat break out on his forehead. He pulled out a handkerchief and wiped it away.

"You're part of the machine-age all right, my dear. You seem able to switch your feelings on and off quite mechanically."

"I don't believe in post-mortems after love-making."

"Good lord," exclaimed Rodney, "Post-mortems are held on dead bodies. Just now you were alive in my arms and you seemed as crazy about me as I am about you. Do passions die so suddenly and completely?"

"You ought to know. But the quick switch isn't a masculine prerogative," she laughed. "Anyhow my passions aren't dead. I want you again right now."

"You do?" He bent down to her eagerly.

Gently she warded him off.

"But no! I don't want to spoil what was so perfect. Not at this moment. You're greedy, Rod. When one finds anything perfect one should savour it – be rather like a gourmet who makes an excellent meal last, and never throws it down his throat, and rushes for a second helping."

"You're terribly logical. I can't cope with you . . ." He broke off and catching both her hands, pressed them to his cheeks and closed his eyes. "Oh, God, I do love you, Perdita. I do – with all my heart."

"Poor Rodney. You mustn't. You've got your family."

"You're determined to make me behave better than I want to do. Ought I to be grateful to you?" He gave a short laugh and dropped her hands as though the touch of them burned him.

"Rodney darling, listen! In my own funny way I am in love with you but I just don't want our affair to become such a big thing in my life that it will eventually take my mind off my work. I know there are men who feel the same way. Why should it be so odd that I do?"

Rodney laughed again and wiped his lips with his handkerchief.

"I need a drink . . ."

"Pour yourself out the wine."

He wished she had some whisky. He needed something stronger than wine but he drank the wine. Then he said:

"It so happens that the average woman *doesn't* feel that way. You are unique, especially as you haven't any other masculine traits. Yes you have – perhaps that cold scientific brain of yours *is* altogether more masculine than feminine. Okay – I'm a mere male, hoist with his own petard."

Perdita laughed quite gaily.

"Isn't that fun? There's a certain sardonic humour in it that appeals to me."

Rodney suddenly dragged the bath-wrap down away from her shoulders and took her in his arms.

"God – how I hate you!"

She laughed again but made no effort to repulse him. On the contrary, she gave herself up to his embrace with a delight which he swore was genuine. While he could feel the pride of possession and enjoy his customary role of the triumphant male, relishing her response, her fervour, he was content. But it was not a role that she allowed him to play for long. Soon he found himself sitting quietly beside her again. This time she was dressed in slacks and jersey and had tied back her glorious hair. He was gripped by an agony of helpless, hopeless passion which was new and confusing to him.

She was charming and friendly, admitted that she loved him and enjoyed his love-making more than she had done with her don. She even agreed that it would be a crime if they were to say goodbye and turn their backs on this mutual passion in which they were so well-matched. Yet he still could not feel that she belonged to him.

"You will let me see you from time to time – be with you like this?" he asked.

"Yes, why not?"

His spirits lifted.

"I couldn't bear it if I couldn't see you again, you know that."

"I think I'd miss you too, Rod. But there's no need for us to separate completely just because you are a married man and I am eventually going to America."

"You can be very cold-blooded, my darling," he said with a short laugh.

Her strange eyes mocked him.

"I bet you've been the same, at times, with your girl-friends. But men today are learning fast that they can't be the only ones to call the tune. And quite right too! Personally, I think the poor little creature so madly in love with an egotistical man that she crawls around him begging for crumbs, is both pathetic and undesirable. Thank goodness there aren't many of them left."

He fastened darkly on the idea of her going to America.

"One day," he said, "you'll get married. You've said so. Okay, it's going to be *to me.*"

"Who said that?"

"I did. You'll never be a poor little creature begging for crumbs, but you want me as much as I want you, and I know it."

Even as he said those words he knew that he had made a mistake. That lovely face of hers hardened and the smile she gave him now was without tenderness.

"Typical man, darling. You take a lot for granted. If we married, we'd fight like anything. We'd get on terribly well in bed. We both like music, and we'd have a lot of fun going round the world together. But we're not soul-mates. You're not really the sort of man I want eventually to marry."

"What sort *do* you want. An intellectual?"

"No."

"Someone your own age? You find me too middle-aged for you?"

She took one of his hands and played with it. Her expression was softer.

"Rodney, don't let's analyse and dissect everything like this. It can be dangerous."

"I thought you were an analyst by nature," he said bitterly.

"Of computers – not emotions. I'm really rather scared of them. In my mind they should be separated from sheer physical sensation."

Rodney leaned forward and pulled a cigarette from a half-opened packet. As he tapped one on his thumb-nail he stared sombrely at the floor; then at his watch. Quarter to one in the morning. Time had stood still. Perdita's lips and beautiful body had burned away all remembrance of his old life.

But now, suddenly, he remembered that he would have to become the old Rodney and return to the old life with Fran and his son.

"You're very quiet," said Perdita.

He tried to laugh.

"As the Americans say, I'm still 'in shock'."

"Maybe you want something to eat, my poor darling."

He suddenly agreed that he was hungry, and that as it was much too late for him to take her out to dinner, they would have to find some food here in the flat.

"I'll cook you egg and bacon," said Perdita and stood up, stretching her arms above her head.

His gaze swept up and down the lithe, tall, magnificent body. He too, stood up and put both hands on her shoulders.

"At least until you go away, will you promise to go on seeing me and let me come here like this again?"

"If it's possible, but the girls are very rarely away together."

"I go over to Paris," he said eagerly. "If you could join me there, it would be terrific – even for twenty-four hours. I have a very important French client I have to see at times and could go without raising any eyebrows at home."

Perdita gave him a long curious look, then shook her head.

"No wonder I dread marriage. Men like you don't seem to have any scruples about being faithless to your wives."

"All right," Rodney said savagely, "I haven't scruples. Fran is a very good person and a devoted wife but I haven't been in love with her for a long time. It's mostly my fault, no doubt, but that's the way it is. I can't help it."

"I'm sorry," said Perdita.

"Does it worry you? Are you going to let the existence of my wife trouble your conscience?"

"Not exactly. But I could only go on seeing you this way if I thought it could be kept a secret. Between us. I wouldn't want to upset your wife. You have a son, too. I don't think it's good for children to end up with divorced parents and broken homes."

"There's no chance of that," he said bitterly – "but, my God, you do tie up all the loose ends meticulously, don't you?"

"It's better, before this sort of thing can develop. It saves a lot of trouble if one knows exactly where one is going, and can stay the course."

"My God," said Rodney again. "I've never thought it possible for any woman to be so – so —"

"So what?"

She moved near him then and of her own free will kissed his mouth. She said:

"There's something about you that I find terribly attractive. I don't deny it. But if we're to go on being lovers, let's do it tidily. It's the only way, I *could* agree to having an affair with you, or any married man."

"Well, it's not going to be any man *but* me."

She gave a little cry and drew back from him.

"You're hurting me. You don't know how strong you are."

"You're the strong one. And by God I love you!" he said.

"I'm not sure I believe in love."

"Don't be cynical."

"That's fine, coming from you."

Was he cynical? He supposed so. He was certainly no longer the careless, carefree sort of chap he used to be, before Miranda died.

Suddenly for the first time he told Perdita about Miranda.

This time she sat at his feet, her arms folded around her hunched knees, looking up at him with those blue disturbing eyes. They were the eyes of a woman who was not going to let a man get away with pretence. Above all, Perdita demanded the truth.

"You reminded me of her – at least the colour of your eyes and the texture of your hair. I thought when I first saw you – if Miranda had grown up, she might have looked a little like you. Perhaps not so tall. She was small for her age."

Perdita's expression had softened while she listened. She gave a clicking sound, with her tongue against her cheek.

"How grim! Poor little thing! And it's happened so many times. People will keep pools and lakes within reach of tiny children."

"We meant to have that one drained if we'd taken the place," he said heavily.

"It must have been bad for you – losing your little daughter, but for her mother – it was appalling. What *she* must have suffered, poor thing!"

He felt almost jealous of her sympathy for Fran. He said nothing. But Perdita read his thoughts. She continued:

"Yes, it was worse for her. Think of it – turning her back only for a moment or two – then coming back to that terrible sight. It must have nearly killed her."

Suddenly he was ashamed because he had so often thought of his own grief and not Fran's.

"It was hell for her. I admit it."

"But you were never quite the same to her after. Is that the way of it?"

He flushed crimson. Perdita was too diabolically clever. He tried to argue himself out of this truth before her cool critical gaze, but he finally gave in.

"Yes, I suppose I've been a bastard to Fran from time to

time. I tried not to show my feelings, but I was so hard-hit, it did seem to come between us. We never talk about it now – but we are not – lovers – as we used to be."

"Men seem strangely unable to feel sorry for anyone but themselves," said Perdita, and shrugged as though bored by her own philosophy.

Rodney sprang to his feet.

"Why the hell are you so friendly with me? You despise me."

She looked up at him and shook her head.

"I don't. You are very touchy, Rod – just a spoilt baby. I've never really liked children. I wouldn't know how to deal with them. They're not my 'thing', but somehow I feel I've got to try and deal with you – you're such a mixed-up kid!"

He exploded.

"Good God, what are you going to call me next? Why did I ever tell you about Miranda?"

She stood up, and taking his arm between her two long fine hands, kissed his cheek.

"Poor Rod! I understand better than I did. It's the father-complex that has drawn you to me because you think your poor little girl might have looked like me. I'm sorry if I've been horrid to you. There's something in me that makes me like that, and I can't bear people who are sorry for themselves."

"No," he said, "all the sympathy is due to Fran, my wife, I agree. I'm a rotten character. I think I'd better go home."

She lifted a hand and ran it through his thick goldenish hair, then with a forefinger traced the outline of the scowling brows and sulky, handsome mouth.

"Darling, you're so good-looking. And so silly. Can't you see that this is not all one-sided? I need you just as much as you do me. You have come into my life at a time when I had begun to be afraid I was too much like a machine, myself. I need to be loved, too – to relax as I did just now in your arms. Don't let's spoil what's between us by thinking about what happened in the past or might happen in the future. That's the way to break up any love-affair. Let's just take what we're offered and as long as we don't hurt your wife – and I presume she needn't know about us – let's be happy together, when we can."

He gave a cry and dragged her into his arms and caressed her madly, feverishly, feeling that he was suspended in mid-air, caught between ice and fire, between right and wrong, between heaven and hell, and he no longer cared about Fran or Peter or anybody in the world except Perdita.

The temptation with her was too great.

He went back to his house in the early hours of the morning, feeling drained of all feeling other than the outstanding desire to possess completely this extraordinary girl. He knew that eventually she would leave him. He was almost sure that her need for him was physical rather than mental, but it was enough that she seemed to need him so much now.

And that was how it all began.

How it would end, he neither knew nor cared. They had become lovers, and lovers he intended they should remain for as long as it was possible.

At that time, he had not the slightest intention of leaving Fran and Peter. The total break-up of his marriage had never entered his head. And when he thought about it, he took it for granted that however he, personally, felt about things, Perdita would not want a permanent relationship with him. He was, however, not blind to the possibility that their relationship as it stood, was dynamite. If it exploded, it would wreck not only his wife, his son and their home, but perhaps, Perdita, too. He was certain she was not as impregnable as she thought. Her disposition suggested that she could handle any situation and that it would leave her untouched. But there was bound to be a chink in the armour somewhere, he thought. And once her defences were down, her destruction might even be more complete than if she had been a more ordinary sort of girl.

9

Now he had to face Fran.

By the time she came home he had made an effort to reorientate himself and be more considerate than usual. As far as he could make out she seemed content. She was without complexities – she was a simple feminine creature – the kind Perdita could never be – wrapped up in her home, her husband, and her child.

He congratulated himself that he played his part well and did not let her guess that he had deviated from the path of virtue while she was away. She could not know that he was madly in love with a young girl – almost young enough to be his own daughter.

So life went on. The summer slipped by and when Rodney went over to Paris on two separate occasions during the months that followed, Perdita managed to be there, with him.

If she had no use for his mentality and was interested only in their physical relationship, Rodney accepted the fact. He was so crazily in love. The days and nights spent in her company seemed glorious. She was a generous lover, shut away with him in their small hotel – right away from that part of Paris in which he might run into friends or acquaintances. Perdita didn't know Paris and he had the pride and pleasure of showing her the beautiful city. They walked everywhere. Perdita was a great walker, and it was something new and pleasurable for Rodney because Fran had a weak back and was quickly tired. They nearly always drove around sight-seeing when they were on holiday.

It was only at the end of these hectic stolen weekends that Rodney began to suffer. He could not bear to leave Perdita. He disliked having to go back to Fran and act a part, and often found it difficult to get on top of his ill-humour and keep the truth from her. He found himself beginning to resent the honest and affectionate expression in her eyes. It made him feel guilty. He loathed being made to feel that way. In some perverted fashion this feeling became misdirected against Fran herself. He began to resent her because she stood between Perdita and himself. But for her and the boy, he could stay with Perdita. He was never really sure that he possessed Perdita except during those hours when she slept with him, and then he knew full well that they shared a mad kind of joy which now neither one could do without.

The very existence of Peter upset Rod. He was well aware that he neglected his paternal duties and was always being begged by Fran to write the weekly letter or go down to a Sports Day, or some other such burdensome event. And of course it shouldn't be a burden. Peter should be his pride and joy, and oh God, if Miranda had lived, he would have *wanted* to be a good father to *her*. It was all wrong and he was all mixed up. And Fran, poor Fran, got the worst of it.

They began to quarrel openly. He knew perfectly well most of it was his fault. But Fran had started to nag and that was more than his frayed nerves would stand.

"*Why won't you do this?*"

"*Why won't you do that?*"

"*Why aren't you like Bill who is so nice to his wife or Leslie who is such a wonderful father?*"

"*Why, why, why?*"

And on the other side of the '*why's*' completely unknown to Fran, of course, there stood the tall golden figure of Perdita, mocking him with her cold blue gaze, and her lazy voice, whispering her own '*why's*' in his ear, as she lay in his arms:

"Why are you such a bastard, darling? You do treat your family shockingly. Why do I let you? Why do I want you so much? I've always made it my policy to get what I want, at any price. So here we are."

Rodney did not try any longer to give her up. He existed now only for the hours spent with her. He suffered from almost uncontrollable jealousy because he did not know what she did in the life she spent apart from him. She baffled and destroyed him.

On one occasion – it was a fine June evening – he made one

of his increasingly frequent excuses to Fran, and drove Perdita down to Bray for dinner.

She was in a dark mood. He had learned that she was not always as placid, as immovable as he had imagined. She could flare up suddenly and unexpectedly into cold rages. Yes, even her rages were cold. But the things she said were often biting, even cruel.

Rodney was rapidly learning what it meant to toe the line. He had never done so in his life before. Neither his mother nor his wife would have recognised this new Rodney. They had seemed content in the past to occupy a deferential position. Now it was he who deferred to Perdita – who was apprehensive of upsetting her, of losing her. More than anything of boring her.

On this particular night he had booked dinner at The Hind's Head – her choice. She waited till they were half-way there, then in a rather sullen voice, said:

"When we go out, I don't like going to places where you take your wife. Why didn't you tell me you brought her here?"

When he had asked, surprised, why she should worry about Fran, Perdita flared up.

"Oh, I have my own type of conscience – or call it what you like. And there are a few delicacies I like to preserve. Let's stick to *our* haunts and not go to those connected with your wife."

He was quite happy about this but she was silent and preoccupied for the rest of the drive. He let well alone and made no attempt to talk to her. But he thought of Fran.

He had only once taken Fran down to Bray – long ago. Neither of them were really keen on the river. As a boy, Rodney had favoured sailing and he and Fran generally migrated to the sea when they wanted an outing. More often than not of course, it was the Eastbourne Road for them, with his mother at the end of it.

Perdita knew that he had a mother, but did not want to know more, neither had she ever asked him to describe his wife or thc life he led with her.

Sometimes he felt that Perdita had a more masculine side to her than the average woman. He had never known one so capable of putting her emotional life on a shelf and taking it down only when it was wanted. Different, indeed, from Fran who could melt at a touch from his hand and who used to angle in a purely feminine way for his attentions. As for his conscience –what little he had left was fast vanishing.

Perdita quarrelled with him during the meal at Bray.

"I oughtn't to be here really. I skipped a lecture because you insisted on taking me out," she said ungraciously.

Rodney abandoned the lobster which he had been enjoying, and looked at her classic, marvellous face with its frame of shining hair. He answered:

"My dear girl, I didn't mean to *drag* you here for dinner. You should have explained that you preferred to go to the lecture."

Her blue eyes narrowed, glittered at him through the dark lashes which he found so attractive in so fair a woman.

"Oh, you know what you're like. You never do understand the importance of my work and you make such a fuss if I break an appointment. I had to come with you."

"I deny that you had to. You never have to do anything you don't want. You know that."

"Oh well, skip it," she said briefly.

He was thunderstruck. It was the first time that she had spoken so harshly to him. He didn't understand it; and he was annoyed.

"Quite frankly, darling, I don't find it particularly amusing taking you out if that's how you feel."

"Skip it," she repeated. "Let's try and enjoy our meal now we're here."

"If we have to *try* to enjoy being together, we might as well call it a day," said Rodney, and instantly regretted it. Perdita wasn't the kind of girl you could say that sort of thing to and get away with it. She immediately agreed with what he had said.

He lit a cigarette. His fingers shook. His *amour propre* had received a considerable jolt. He hadn't imagined that Perdita could be quite so casual. At the same time he was reminded painfully of a scene played in reverse between Fran and himself some time ago. She had accused him of not wanting to make love to her any more – it wasn't often that Fran lowered her pride to that extent, but she had let herself go that night. It was she who had said: '*If that's all you care for me nowadays we'd better call it a day*,' and he, with a coldness amounting to indifference (like Perdita's) had agreed. But a few minutes later, Fran had clung to him weeping and he, remorseful, had comforted her and it was all over.

Perdita, however, had no comfort for Rodney.

"You know, I have tried to avoid love-affairs because people make such demands on each other when they are what is called 'going steady'. I've always thought it better to love and ride away, and I'm sure that's what *you've* done in the past. I can't think why you make such issues of everything with us. It's so boring."

Rodney stared at her, then signalled to the waiter for the bill. Though he was completely in love with this girl, he was now deeply hurt and offended. Nobody – nobody before had ever called him a bore. When they got into the Mercedes to drive home, Perdita, with astonishing unconcern, began to hum an aria from Figaro. Rodney listened gloomily, his fingers gripping the wheel with nervous strength. He remembered how they had enjoyed that record in her flat. Both lovers of that particular Mozart opera. Both *lovers*. But tonight he could hardly believe she had ever lain in his arms and explored with him the intimacies of passionate love. She could *hum* while he brooded and suffered, he thought. She, a young girl . . . God what a volte-face for him. He was furiously indignant.

As they drew up outside her flat, he said briefly:

"It's started to rain. I believe I've got an old umbrella in the back. Take it. Your hair will get wet."

She laughed and spoke good-naturedly now:

"Darling Rod! I don't mind if I get my hair wet or not. It's time I washed it, anyhow."

"Well, good-night," he said heavily.

Then suddenly she seemed to thaw. She was all woman

again, laying a hand on his knee, pressing it, and rubbing her cool fragrant cheek against his.

"You really are a silly old thing."

He gave a short laugh.

"Too old and too silly for you, my child, that's obvious."

"I used the old as a term of affection. You don't really seem old to me. As I've told you before, you're really very young, in spite of being nearly forty; a big handsome well-to-do stock-broker with a family."

He winced.

"That sounds deadly. No wonder you're bored."

The rain was coming down hard. He bent forward and with a duster wiped the mist from the windscreen. She took his hands now and placed them against her long throat. She knew it fascinated him to feel the beat of the pulse there when he pressed it.

"Rodney, why are we quarrelling? You know I love you in my funny way."

"Well, it's a *damned* funny way."

"Only when you start getting all het up and pompous. I don't like scenes."

"Allow me to remind you that I was perfectly all right when we first met. It was you who was in a bad mood."

"That's quite true," said Perdita. "I admit I was feeling frustrated."

He repeated the word, laughing ironically.

"*You* should be frustrated! What about me?"

"Oh, Rod, why can't you face the facts? Our affair can never be anything but a series of meetings like the one we've had tonight which so easily ends in a ridiculous quarrel."

"Quarrelling with you is the last thing I want. I've had enough of it at home."

"Do you have many rows with your wife?"

This was the first time she had ever made any such enquiry.

He gave an impatient sigh.

"In fairness to Fran, whatever rows there are, are of my making. She's very patient and I'm not easy to live with."

"I'm sure you're not. I'd hate to live with you."

"Yet you sleep with me," he said with a sudden brutal frankness.

Now she pressed his hands against her breasts.

"I enjoy our love-making just as much as you do," she murmured.

He smelled the perfume of her hair and tasted the sweetness of her moist pink mouth.

He could no longer withstand the desire to surrender, yet again, his pride and all of himself to this girl. He took her in his arms and kissed her with crazy passion. The whole spoiled evening was forgotten as he felt the hunger in the response from her mouth.

He couldn't go up with her to the flat tonight. Her girl-friends were both in. All he could do was to repeat and repeat that he didn't care what happened so long as she would love him even for a short while. Her beauty, her youth, her clear disarming intelligence had become essential to his existence.

"Don't leave me. Never leave me," he said violently.

"I'll have to when I get my job abroad," she said, and sighed.

"Then I'll follow you. I don't care what happens at home. I'll tell Fran the truth. My marriage is a farce. I wanted a divorce long ago but I've never had the guts to suggest it."

Perdita drew away from him.

"For God's sake don't do anything like that on my account."

"I can't let you go out of my life," he said, "and nothing you say will make me change my mind about that."

"Well, the situation doesn't arise for the moment," she said, kissed him hard on the mouth and got out of the car. She slammed the door as though to intimate that she did not want him to get out as well, and that their evening was over.

He stared at her through the car window. The rain was pouring down. She seemed oblivious of it. He could see her long blonde hair soaked with it. The smile that she gave him as she turned away told him nothing. It was as enigmatic, he thought, as the curve on the lips of the Mona Lisa.

That was the sort of evening he spent with her on several occasions during the months that followed. He was perfectly happy when they ended the evening in each other's arms. But he felt like a foolish love-sick boy when he could not be with her. In the past all he had wanted was a casual affair, but this one – no. The insecurity from which he suffered at times during their association drove him mad. Certainly she was changing him. His whole disposition was changing. His men friends accused him of becoming morose and difficult. There were times when he cursed his friend George Stirling for ever having introduced him to Perdita Shaw.

Then there was Fran. Fran who said nothing – did nothing –whatever she felt about him. He didn't quite know whether or not she recognised the alteration in him, but he feared that she did and that she suffered from doubts and depression.

The family excursions to Eastbourne to see his mother became an added tax on his patience. Mama was always full of affection and flattery, but he wondered what in God's name she would have said if she had known that he was being systematically unfaithful to his wife, or what Fran would say if he told her that he wanted to leave her. For whatever Perdita felt about things, Rodney had begun to suspect that it was his marriage – and the existence of his son – that really stood between him and Perdita. Every time they made love he became more confident that she did not really want to let him go. He was becoming a necessity in her life. If he had been free she would possibly have encouraged him to go to America with her.

Perdita's future in America became a menace that increased with every week that passed.

10

ONE night in October they entered another phase.

Jacqueline Hurst, the model girl, who shared the flat with Perdita suddenly packed up and left, having had, so Rodney was told, a row with the other tenant, Annabel Kaye. Annabel departed the following week. She was studying for her Finals at London University and had decided to go home and live there quietly until she was through. London life offered too many temptations. She was almost as dedicated to her work as Perdita was to her computer.

Rodney felt elated when he heard that Perdita was now living alone. And when she told him she was about to put an advertisement in the paper in order to find two new girls to share the flat, he begged her not to do so.

"For the love of Mike, let's keep things as they are. You know how difficult it's been getting a single evening absolutely alone. This is a god-given break."

"I know, but I can't afford it," said Perdita.

"But I can," he said eagerly.

They were up there in Perdita's shabby room which for Rodney had become a hundred times more desirable than Fran's beautiful drawing-room. Perdita was in one of her unusually loving and giving moods. They were sharing one of the badly cooked suppers which for Rodney had all the essence of happiness, which he never now criticised even inwardly. Sometimes she wondered how many times he had eaten that dreadful paella – the first dish she had cooked for him last April. Now it was early October. The long golden days of summer had passed. The evenings were drawing in and London was cold and misty in the early morning and late afternoons. The strong odour of burning leaves filled the parks and the brilliance of the dahlias was dimmed, the blooms sodden and spoilt by the incessant rain. The weather was poor this autumn. But it was warm in Perdita's flat with the electric fire full on and Perdita was always warm – Rodney often told her during their love-sessions it was like holding a flame in his arms, all the more fascinating because he knew that there was the cool, aloof woman behind that fire.

"Don't relet those rooms," he coaxed. "Keep the flat just for us."

"I don't see how I can possibly afford the rent," said Perdita.

She was lying on the sofa. He sat on a hassock beside her. She wore the white towelling wrap with which he was now familiar. She had powdered her body and touched her ears and throat with the *Shalimar* perfume he had bought her in Paris. He was fully dressed. Sometimes she accused him of being fundamentally suburban and respectable because he didn't like sitting around *en déshabillé*. He was always elegant, well-tailored; but she liked his sartorial perfection, she said. It was a change from the untidy and badly dressed students who had been her male companions at the University.

Now Rodney dared to suggest that he could well afford the rent if she would allow him to pay it, and keep the flat only for her. Hastily he added that he did not intend it as an insult.

She flung back her magnificent head and laughed.

"How idiotic can you be? Why should I feel offended? You really are too conventional. I'm not in the least averse to being helped with the rent if you want to pay."

"Aren't you?" he asked astonished.

"No, I can pay it back and will do. I'm going to get a very big salary once I'm in America."

Rodney had reached a pitch where he was too infatuated to criticise her for accepting his money. Conversely, it made him feel good. It added to his feeling of power, of possession.

Before he left her that night he gave her a cheque.

She folded it, looking at him with eyes half-shut like blue slits; rather a wicked satirical smile curling her wide pink lips.

"What fun! I've never taken money from anyone – male or female before."

"I'm very happy about it."

"You mean it makes you feel fine – possessive."

"You read my thoughts like a book don't you?"

"Now you look sulky. That down-droop to your lips amuses me. You're very handsome, my pet."

"Oh, shut up!" he said with sudden fury.

She tendered the cheque to him grimacing.

"Take it back?"

He flung himself upon her, kissing her with a violence that made her gasp in protest, then relax.

That was the sort of love-making Perdita enjoyed.

The cheque fluttered to the floor.

For the rest of that month he paid her in cash. He also began to buy her expensive presents. A mink tie for the autumn; a Hartnell suit. She looked magnificent in it. A set of leather-bound books she coveted. This sudden aspect of her character –her willingness to take so much – surprised him. It didn't seem to be in keeping with this girl with her cool trained mind, her independent spirit. But he felt no contempt. She jotted down a memorandum of every pound he gave her. She handed him the small diary to see one evening.

"All correct? You shall have dollar bills which will help you with foreign currency abroad. You can take your good little wife and nice little boy for a ski-ing holiday," she said.

He threw the small book with the exquisitely neat correct figures on to her lap.

"Oh, hell, Perdita, what do you take me for?"

"I've taken you for my lover," she mocked. "Nothing else."

"Well, don't jeer at my wife and son," he snapped, suddenly out of control.

She was standing by the electric fire, warming her fine long hands.

It had been awkward for Rod to get here. Fran had expected him to keep a dinner date they had with the Franklins – old friends from South Africa. He had made the rather feeble – now outworn excuse, that one of his most important clients was passing through London tonight and must be given first refusal.

They had fought about it. Fran was not quite the submissive type she used to be. He knew that the change lay at his door. The old soft tender expression on her face had been replaced by a hostile and even suspicious one. He had grown reckless – careless – hardly caring whether or not she suspected him of having a clandestine affair. She had said:

"You're always making excuses to get away. You seem to hate being with me these days."

He had answered harshly:

"You damned women are all the same – a man has a business date and something else is read into it. You used to be much more intelligent, Fran. I don't know what's got into you."

"And I don't know what's got into *you*," she had flung back at him. "Look at this. It came from Peter this morning, only you wouldn't know."

She handed him a letter. Rod could see that her fingers were trembling and her small face quite red with anger. He scanned Peter's letter. He had good handwriting for a boy of thirteen, and quite a lot to say, Rodney's cheeks burned as he read the paragraph Fran pointed out.

"You said I was to look forward to the Christmas hols but I don't as much as I used to. You and Dad seemed so cross with each other in the summer. What's got into Dad? He's pretty difficult and you seem fed up. Oh, well, I suppose it will be all right. I hope so."

Fran said:

"That's nice, isn't it? Pete's overheard some of our arguments. He's not a baby any more you know. He feels there's something wrong with Dad and something wrong with Mum, too. We're fine parents, making that nice son of ours worried and suspicious."

For a moment Rodney stayed silent. Frozen, furious, because he could not deny what she said, and tormented by his inability to alter things. Finally he had resorted to the coward's way out. Wilde was right – '*the coward does it with a kiss, The brave man wih a sword*', and all that.

He hadn't the courage to tell the truth and use the sword. He didn't really relish wounding Fran or Peter mortally. Yet hadn't he already done it? They were both suffering from the effects his liaison with Perdita had had upon him. He hadn't the guts to leave his family – or Perdita. He was a coward.

True, Perdita had warned him not to break with his family on her account. He was afraid that she might vanish out of his sight for good and all if he disregarded her wishes. So he did nothing. There seemed nothing to do but mark time and carry on with the intrigue, the lies and the hypocrisy. But he knew he had been difficult at home lately. A 'bastard' – that was the word Perdita so often used.

So he had caught hold of Fran, dropped a kiss on her hair and forced a note of apology and remorse into his voice.

"Sorry, darling. I'll write to Pete tonight. I'll say something about us all making preparations to have a great Christmas this year and cheer him up."

Fran turned her face from his kiss and he knew that she was crying. But he dared not stay and be drawn into a sentimental scene. He couldn't stand it. He couldn't take Fran in his arms with genuine love. He had lost all the old desire for her.

"I swear I'll write," he said again, and hurriedly left her.

But he hadn't been able to get away as quickly as he wanted. The telephone-bell rang as he was putting on his overcoat. Fran shouted over the bannisters:

"Rod – it's your mother. She wants to speak to you."

His mother was the last person Rodney wanted to speak to. He was very fond of the old girl but lately she had entered a phrase of perpetual whining. Why didn't he come and see her more often? Why didn't he bring Fran down to Eastbourne on Sundays as he used to do? She was sure something was wrong. She knew her boy. The last time she had seen him he had looked so ill and seemed so nervy, etc., etc.

When he spoke to her, Rod tried to be bright and filial.

"Nice to hear from you, dear. How's our Granny?"

"Not at all well. You must come and see me. The doctor doesn't like my condition."

Rodney had heard this sort of thing before, but he said:

"Sorry about that. What's wrong?"

"I'll tell you when you come. Do make it this Sunday, dear."

He chewed at his lips, racking his brains to remember what had been arranged for Sunday. He had reached a pitch where he found it awkward to make any appointment until he had heard what Perdita wanted to do. She was often free at weekends and it was fortunate for him that Fran, long before he met Perdita, had grown used to visiting his mother without him.

He promised that he would do his best to take Fran to Eastbourne on Sunday. Mrs. Grifford's last words were a trifle disconcerting:

"Dr. Budd wants to see, you, too. I know he will come if you promise to be here about mid-day. I'll give you and Fran lunch afterwards."

So he had had to give the promise. And he had felt a genuine pang of fear for the old lady, wondering if Dr. Budd had anything really serious to tell him. After all, Granny was getting on – seventy-six. Anything might happen at that age. And not even the allure of Perdita could wipe out the affection he had always had for his mother.

Now, in Perdita's flat, he remembered about his mother. He had meant to tell Perdita but she was being particularly disagreeable because he had snapped at her. She turned from the fire, swept back a lock of hair, and twisted her lips at him.

"*Oie . . . yoy . . . oie!*" She gave a lazy imitation of a Jewish lament. "Don't tell me Rodney Grifford is growing sensitive about his family . . ." She stooped and picked up the little account-book . . . "I will pay you back every shilling you've lent me for the rent as soon as I can. I don't want to accept your help and have you dictating what I should or shouldn't say about your wife and son. I was only pulling your leg about the dollars anyhow. You're very touchy all of a sudden."

He lit a cigar, his fingers trembling. He was in a state of jitters and knew it. Since his love-affair with Perdita had started, he had gone to pieces. His work was suffering. The thought of her confused his memory. He had made several mistakes lately in his dealings with clients who mattered. He had an almost insane wish at this moment to throw the whole game up, tell Perdita to go to hell, and walk out of this flat for good and all. Then he thought what that would mean – back to the old dull monotonous matrimonial life – never again to hold this glorious girl in his arms. Never again to feed on the fascination of her extraordinary mind.

Tonight she was being unusually female and even spiteful, but as a rule she had a broad tolerant outlook and he could talk to her as man to man. Then they would end up in delicious abandon, man and woman, hotly, madly desiring, perfectly matched lovers, in circumstances where the mind was not of such importance.

He said:

"Oh, darling, darling, don't let's quarrel tonight. I can't take it. I didn't mean to offend you, for heaven's sake. I just didn't like the way you brought Fran and Peter into the dollar-bill discussion, that's all. I thought you were getting at me.'

"Perhaps I was."

He drew a long deep breath of his cigar, struggling for self-possession, and shut his eyes as the blue smoke curled between them and the room was filled with fragrance. A good cigar always soothed Rodney's nerves. He spoke more calmly.

"Have I done something to deserve it?"

She yawned.

"Oh God, don't you have plenty of arguments at home? Surely you don't come here just to carry on with them?"

He put the cigar down in an ashtray, walked up to her, and pulled her into his arms.

"It's the last thing I want. I hate arguing with you. This sort of acrimonious conversation only starts when we're both tired out and one misconstrues something the other has said."

She relented.

"I oughtn't to be horrid to you," she murmured, and relaxed against him, her cheek against his. "You're so very good to me. I was beastly about the cheque and I had no right to mention your holiday with your family."

Later when their shared passion was spent and she was making coffee for him, he said:

"My God, it's good to look at you now and see that I can still make you happy. You glow from head to foot. Your skin – your hair – marvellous! They *glow*. And it's marvellous to think that this flat is our own now – a place nobody else can share. It's an oasis for me, darling, darling Perdita."

She handed him a cup of coffee and while he stirred it, sat at his feet and became the utterly feminine glorious woman who so completely enslaved him.

He got home in the early hours of the morning, a man exhausted but content. But the contentment vanished when he saw that the light was still on in Fran's bedroom. Although he tiptoed up the stairs, she must have heard him come in. She called to him.

"Rod!"

He stifled a yawn, straightened his tie, and looked in the upstairs gilt-framed mirror that hung on the landing just outside Fran's door. Must make sure there was no powder on his coat. He brushed it hurriedly and walked into his wife's room.

"It's late. I thought you'd be asleep, dear."

"Come in. I want to speak to you," she said. And she spoke so coldly that he hunched his shoulders uncomfortably and scowled. God grant Fran didn't want to start getting at him over nothing at *this* hour. It was past one o'clock.

Of course, he had wanted to stay with Perdita all night. It would have been so easy now she was sole tenant of her flat. But he could hardly expect Fran to believe that his client had wanted to stay out much later than this.

He walked up to Fran's bed with a jaunty air and sat down.

"Not sleeping well these nights, are you? Must get hold of some sleeping pills."

"I've been taking them for the last six weeks but you wouldn't know," she said in that new cold voice which he had never heard from her before.

He glanced at her. She looked very small and thin after Perdita with her Junoesque proportions. Rodney, who of late had not looked at his wife closely noticed tonight that the table-lamp lit up a face that had grown bony and haggard. With a shock he realised that Fran was beginning to look her age – and more. She might have been over forty. He used to tell her, when her eyes were bright and she was laughing, and her hair a little wind-swept and she was wearing jeans and shirt on holiday, that she might be Pete's elder sister rather than his mother. But not tonight.

"Of course I've seen your pills," he mumbled in reply to her accusation, "but I didn't know what they were for."

"They were given to me by Dr. Oliver Pars," she said in a high clear voice. "I told Oliver that I felt so ill and so het-up I thought I might be on the edge of a nervous breakdown. And as I am not the type to enjoy breakdowns, I thought I'd better get some sleep, *somehow*, however het-up I felt."

Rodney loosened his tie and pulled it off. His brows met in a scowl.

"What's this all meant to be – a thing against me? Have you and Oliver been getting together without telling me?"

"Why not? He's a very good doctor and he happens to be mine – ours if you prefer it. But I didn't think you'd be interested. I would remind you that we have been leading separate lives ever since Pete and I came back from Jersey."

Now Rodney fingered the tie nervously. For the first time he felt uneasy about his relationship with his wife. She had never been a very forceful character and rarely tried to impose her personality, wishes, or views upon him. He had liked that. And if it came down to hard facts, Fran was, in her way, a 'yes-girl'. An ideal wife for Rodney Grifford.

But tonight she seemed suddenly to have broken through the usual façade of quiet submission. He had truly believed that she was not unhappy. He was an insensitive type of man, and of course, they had ever-increasing rows. But he always got the better of her and she was always the one to say 'sorry'. Then he acted the magnanimous, all-forgiving husband ready to accept an apology – or even give one if he thought it would keep her quiet. But looking back, he had to admit that Pete had become a constant bone of contention at which they had both been snapping and biting.

But did she suspect that her husband was having an affair? He couldn't believe that. Only the other night when she had accused him of breaking too many appointments and leaving her too much alone, he had talked her down.

"For lord's sake, surely a man ought to have some life of his own; I'm not a sissy. You're much more sentimental than I am, anyhow, and always have been, Fran. And surely I haven't neglected you all that much? Look at Bob Widdowson who is always leaving his wife alone."

She didn't, of course, want to 'look at Bob Widdowson'. He was the one man they both knew who was openly deceiving his wife. Fran then reminded Rod bitterly that Bob had almost had a suicide on his hands. There had been a scandal about Irene Widdowson. She had taken an overdose of sleeping tablets, but lucky for Bob they had found her in time.

A very real twinge of conscience gripped at Rodney's vitals as he remembered this episode. He wished he hadn't brought up old Bob's name. Damned tactless of him. It worried him, too, when he looked at the little bottle by Fran's bed. She followed his gaze and gave what he thought an unnatural laugh.

"Oh, so you remember! Well, of course, some men *are* responsible for killing their wives in the nicest possible way. I, personally, wouldn't dream of committing suicide; not only because I think it's a cowardly way out but because of my son. But . . ." Fran took the bottle and shook it. The little pills rattled against the glass. "I can see now how poor Irene felt, even though I criticised her at the time."

Rodney stopped fidgeting with his tie and stared at his wife. Fear suddenly laid a cold finger upon him. He stuttered:

"I don't know what you're talking about. You don't happen to be in Irene's position."

But I am in the same position, she thought in anguish, *I know I am.*

11

RODNEY drove the Mercedes slowly out of Golders Green and through the traffic down Park Road, heading toward Eaton Square.

It was the third of November and pouring with intermittent sleet and rain. It was also several degrees colder.

Fran sat beside him, huddled in her fur coat. She pulled the black beret she was wearing off her head and shook back her hair. Neither of them had exchanged a word since they left the crematorium.

They had just attended the funeral of old Mrs. Grifford.

Fran's mind was not on this miserable event. She was thinking about Rodney's betrayal of her. She had discovered the existence of his girl-friend by one of those silly accidents.

She was rung up one morning by a jeweller in Bond Street. He had asked first of all if it was Mr. Rodney Grifford's house, apologised for troubling her, then said that Mr. Grifford had asked him to deliver some earrings which they had made for his wife. He had given them an address in Chelsea. But when the messenger got to this flat he found it locked and empty and was told by a next-door neighbour that the owner had gone away. Then the jeweller, who was young and possessed of no tact, thinking he had made a mistake in the address, looked Mr. Rodney Grifford up in the telephone-book and found the address in Eaton Square. So he thought he should have sent the earrings there.

"I think you'll be pleased with your choice, Mrs. Grifford," he had said. "I'll send the box round to you straight away. They're the finest aquamarine and diamond drops we have ever made. You agreed when you came in that they were exquisite stones, didn't you?"

"Did I?" Fran had enquired innocently.

"Yes, that day you came in with Mr. Grifford, or am I not speaking to *Mrs. Grifford*? Oh, I'm so sorry – er – ahem!"

He was obviously worried then, but Fran, seized with a horrible curiosity, had drawn him on.

"Do put me in the picture. My memory is at fault. Was it *I* who came with Mr. Grifford to choose the earrings?"

"Yes, madam, and if you don't mind me reminding you, he mentioned that the colour of the stones (ahem) matched your eyes."

"You're speaking to the wrong person," Fran said, stifling an hysterical wish to burst into laughter, "but I'll tell my husband to collect the earrings. Goodbye."

She told Rodney.

At that time, Rodney, still self-confident, determined to get out of any predicament and carry on with his affair in secret, denied stoutly that he had ever ordered the jewels.

"I'll go round to the shop and wring the fellow's neck for

worrying you, darling," he had said. "The damned earrings must have been ordered by someone else. The chap in Chelsea."

She hadn't believed him, but she had decided not to precipitate a fatal catastrophe. She would lie low and watch. Not that she was the spying kind but it had been such a shock to her to realise that Rodney was buying jewellery for another woman – a woman with eyes that matched the aquamarines – she had wanted time to think. She still loved Rodney to the point of anguish. He was her husband and Peter's father. She wasn't going to let any girl with aquamarine eyes snatch him from her. Perhaps, in any case, he would grow tired of this affair and want to return fully to her, his wife.

But that was only while Fran had still felt him to be worth fighting for. So for a time, she silently and wretchedly watched and waited.

She did not dream of going to a detective and having her husband followed. She knew that in a cowardly way she really did not *want* to know. And she kept her suspicions to herself. She would never have confided in any of her woman friends. She suffered intensely, proudly, and alone.

One night when Rodney came home late and she heard him open the door to his dressing-room, she got out of her bed and opened her own door.

"Oh, hullo," he said, but looked away almost at once as though he preferred not to see her.

"You're very flushed," said Fran, and pursed her lips at him.

"It was hot in the restaurant," he muttered.

"You must have done some heavy drinking – you and your client. It's long past twelve."

"Does a man have to account to his wife for every hour he stays out?"

"Oh, not at all," said Fran with a high theatrical laugh. "You can do just as you like."

"Thanks," he said, "and now if you don't mind I'll get to bed because —"

"Because you're so tired," she broke in with a sarcasm that made Rodney's face go a darker red than it had been before.

There was guilt written all over him, Fran thought, and with sudden seething jealousy convulsing her she turned, walked back into her own room, and slammed the door.

She had to sit down on her bed quickly because she was shaking so badly. She despised herself for that exhibition of rage, and she remembered it now as she sat in the car beside Rodney after her mother-in-law's funeral.

That had been another of many unpleasant scenes – days and nights when they argued and bickered, and she became more and more certain that Rodney was being unfaithful to her.

For a short time after Mrs. Grifford's heart attack – her last few weeks spent in an Eastbourne Nursing Home – the atmosphere had cleared a little. Rodney had shown genuine sorrow because he had been fond of the old lady, and he was kinder to Fran. There had even been a moment when she told him that his mother had died, that he had put his head against her shoulder, and they had cried together and she had comforted him.

He did not go out that night. He stayed with Fran and was more like the old Rod. She had been almost happy again. But the happiness was short-lived. Deflated and depressed again, Fran felt that the end was in sight. She believed that the existence of Rodney's mother while she was alive, had been something of a stabilising influence on him. Now that he no longer need account to the old lady for anything he did, he might go all out to get his freedom.

Her fears were redoubled on the day before the funeral. A new row flared up between them. Peter was the innocent cause. He had an accident on his bicycle at his school. The local doctor put four stitches in his upper lip; and one tooth was knocked out. Matron assured Fran that all was well but Fran felt that she wanted to rush down and see the boy. She asked Rodney to go with her.

He refused.

"A couple of stitches and a missing tooth are not critical. You make a lot too much fuss over him."

"And you don't make enough," Fran returned bitterly.

They had just finished dinner and were drinking coffee. Rodney had been restless all evening, walking up and down, staring into the fire, switching on the television, switching it off again, making it obvious that he was in a state of nerves. In her bitterness Fran had wondered whether it was because of poor Granny's imminent cremation or because he wanted to get out to *that other woman.*

They bickered and argued about Peter. Fran was indignant because she knew she did not spoil Pete but that Rodney was never very affectionate to his son. After half an hour of exchanging reproaches and making all the petty accusations common to married couples who are no longer getting on, Fran lost her temper. It took a lot to make that happen, but when she did – she lost it properly. She screamed at him:

"I've had enough of this. You've been absolutely beastly to me lately – yes, to me, as well as Pete."

"Oh, stop nagging. It's your fault, anyhow."

She shouted.

"It isn't true! You know it. I used to adore you. I used to do anything you wanted. But you stopped loving me after Miranda died."

"You imagine things. We shouldn't talk about Miranda."

"Yes, we should. For years you've kept it all underneath and held it against me and I've never dared breathe her name, but now we will. You loved her much more than you ever loved Peter and you've always blamed me for her death!"

Rodney was shaking. The sweat glistened on his forehead. Oddly enough, in that heated hour, he remembered something that Perdita had said when he told her about the little girl who had drowned in the lily pond.

'*It must have been bad for you . . . but for her mother it was appalling . . .*'

And later:

'*Men seem strangely unable to feel sorry for anyone but themselves.*'

In the middle of this unpleasant scene, how odd that he should remember something *she* had said.

He calmed down.

"For God's sake don't drag *that* up, Fran. I told you after it happened and we'd all calmed down, that I didn't blame you. I know it was an accident."

"But you did hold it against me!" Fran was sobbing – out of control. "You hated me for it. You've hated me for years. You wished Peter had died instead of Miranda. Oh, you would have rushed down to see her if *she* had been injured at school, wouldn't you? *One* stitch would have been enough. Oh, I *hate you.*" She broke off, knuckles pressed against her eyes, her body jerking convulsively.

Rodney was silenced. Fran had never behaved like this before. He had no idea how to cope with her. At the same time, his patience was coming to an end. He had long ago given up holding Miranda's death against Fran. His present hostility toward her sprang from the knowledge that she stood between him and his desire to go to Perdita. But he could not see Fran in this state. He was not indifferent to her suffering. He spoke in a would-be friendly voice.

"Try to pipe down, Fran, for God's sake, and stop talking about Miranda."

There was a long pause. Fran turned from him, blowing her nose. He tried to take her arm, but she shook off his hand. She whispered:

"You'd better be careful. I know more than you think."

"I don't know what you mean."

"Yes, you do. You've got some woman somewhere – a young girl perhaps. The one with the aquamarine eyes. You lied about those earrings. You *did* order them for a girl, didn't you?"

He was defeated and silenced again. She looked up at the face that no longer seemed the charming boyish face of the man she had loved so devotedly. It was red, rather puffy, self-indulgent; the face of the man he had become.

The silence between them was as bitter as gall.

Then Rodney said:

"I think *you'd* better be careful, too, Fran. *Very* careful."

She gave an hysterical laugh.

"Don't you want me to talk about the girl with the eyes as blue as aquamarines? I've laughed about it lots of times."

"Then you'd better go on laughing," said Rodney, and turned and walked out of the room.

Fran flung herself on to the sofa and cried long and miserably. She heard the front door slam. Rodney had gone out. Possibly, she thought, to the girl-friend.

She was almost past caring. She only knew that it was a terrible thing that they should have had a scene like this before poor Granny was even laid to rest. The quarrel had blown up and developed into something terrible before either of them were aware of it. But that Rodney was as guilty as hell, she now believed. She stopped crying, went up to her bedroom, and sat on the edge of her bed. She thought not of herself but of Peter. Peter telling her about that other boy at Prep. School whose parents had been divorced. How awful he had thought it! He had told her at the time how he had gone to the Headmaster and tried to help. Peter was so sensitive. He would loathe his parents to separate. In his way he looked up to his father, and he would hate not to have him around any more. It struck Fran that whatever it cost her in pride or tears, she would not let Rodney go – certainly not while Peter was still at school. What happened when he was older was different.

She did not hear Rodney come home. She had in any case locked her door, unwilling to face him again that night.

In the morning she gave him his coffee and toast and a note, then walked out of the room without so much as bidding him good morning.

She had written:

"*Please agree that there should be no repetition of last night and that if we have to discuss things again it should be like adults, not screaming adolescents.*

"*I apologise for losing my temper. Let us please see there is peace in the house, at least until your mother is buried.*

Fran."

He came upstairs before he went to the office, and spoke to her. A quick glance showed her that he looked ghastly. She wondered if he had had any sleep at all and what lay in that strange selfish mind of his – what devil was tormenting him and leading him on toward the destruction of his wife, his home, his son, and, perhaps, himself.

"I entirely agree with your note, Fran. I'm sorry I was so rough," he said.

That was all. And now poor Granny was dead – and reduced to ashes.

Once home from Golders Green this morning, they had the morbid task of entertaining a few distant cousins who had attended the funeral, and later the family solicitor who had made Granny's Will. She had little to leave except some jewellery which was to be Fran's, and afterwards given to Peter's wife. Of course, her death meant that Rod would be the richer for the allowance he had made his mother during her lifetime.

That night Rodney stayed in. He said he had a lot of letters to write. During the evening meal he and Fran had exchanged few words beyond desultory mention of Rodney's mother and the disposal of her things at the hotel.

Fran said that she would go down and see to everything.

"Give everything away that isn't of value," Rodney said. "She did have her own bed and armchair down there, didn't she? Send them to some second-hand dealer in Eastbourne. All I want you to bring me are her papers, and have that little satinwood bureau which was the only decent thing she had, sent up to us."

"I'll see to it," said Fran. "Where are you going to put it?"

"Oh, somewhere," he said vaguely, "but I remember it as a boy – I always remember Mama using it."

Fran looked at him through her lashes. What a contradictory nature he had! More often than not so insensitive, and yet suddenly tender, sentimental, like this. As he had been about Miranda. Oh God, she thought, if only Miranda had lived! If only she hadn't left her for that moment – that terrible moment. How quickly a baby can die!

How awful that so long afterward the memory should rise to the surface again and strike at the very roots of her being. But she spoke to Rodney gently.

"I'm sure you'll miss your mother. Poor Rod! It's been a sudden shock. I feel it, too."

"Oh, well," said Rodney with a short laugh. "At least it means that you won't have to trek down to Eastbourne again.

"I never really minded. And she adored you – and Peter."

"She was very fond of you, and rightly. You did a lot more for her than I ever did, and, I thank you."

Fran shut her eyes. Tears were forcing their way through her lashes. She felt very unnerved and lonely tonight. And she had never felt more dissociated from her husband. It was all so wrong. This was a night when she should have gone to sleep with his arms around her, comforting her, and she should have comforted him. She fully believed that he was in need of it. If only there wasn't that other woman. Fran was seized with a mad curiosity to know more about her but she tightened her lips and walked out of the room, rather than risk another showdown with Rodney on the night of his mother's funeral.

For the next two or three weeks there was peace in the house. An uneasy peace. But neither of them was at each other's throats, and they both seemed fully occupied. They met only for meals. It took Fran several days to see to the disposal of her mother-in-law's effects in Eastbourne.

So far as Rodney and the 'other woman' were concerned, she noticed that he certainly did not go out as often as usual. He cancelled only one social engagement Fran had made for them.

Meanwhile they lived together under the same roof like strangers; formal, polite to one another.

Their best friends, Harriet and Ted Lock came round to dinner and tried to line them up to share a trip to the West Indies during December.

Fran left Rodney to answer. To her relief he refused the invitation. She, herself, didn't want to go away just then. But after the Locks had gone and she was in bed, Fran lay wondering wretchedly why Rod had been so quick to turn down the offer. The old Rod would have accepted it. He had always been anxious to see Jamaica and Ted was one of his best friends. Added to which, it was a sterling area. They need have no currency problem.

The Locks had said they would be home before Christmas. Pete didn't break up till the 20th, so it must be that Rodney did not want to go abroad and leave *her* . . . the mysterious girl who had come between them.

But Rodney continued to behave as though such a person did not exist.

Fran hid her haggard face against the pillow and wept. What was happening to her once happy marriage? Where were all the old faith and trust and love?

What was happening to Rod?

How long was she going to have to carry on before he came into the open and told her the truth?

12

PETER came home for Christmas full of the enthusiasm he usually showed at this season. And whatever Rodney was doing in private, he volunteered to stay home that evening for a celebration meal, and was particularly nice to Peter.

He grinned at the thin, lanky, dark-eyed boy and slapped him on the back.

"You're growing too damned fast – stop it! I refuse to have a son taller than myself."

"Oh gosh, Dad, I've got a long way to go till then," Peter laughed.

"He'll never be tall. He takes after me and my side of the family," put in Fran.

Peter turned to her and puffed out his lips.

"My accident doesn't show any more, does it, Mum?"

Fran examined the lip.

"Just a tiny scar. He must be a jolly good surgeon, but we'll have to get that tooth put in. I'll ring up Mr. Wheeler."

"And don't go falling off any more bicycles," added Rodney.

"Dad," said Peter eagerly, "my friend Stephen Wallace is

keen on stamps. His father's a well-known philatelist, too. Steve's lent me his best collection and I want to try and improve mine. Would you like to have a look at Steve's?"

It had been on the tip of Rodney's tongue to say that the one hobby that bored him most was collecting stamps, but he caught Fran's eye. He let his son down lightly.

"Sometime – yes. But I'm rather busy just now.'

"Okay," said Peter.

After his father had left the room, Peter looked at his mother.

"I say, Mum, Dad's being rather super these hols. Why the change?"

Fran caught her lower lip between her teeth and felt her cheeks redden. Such a question highly embarrassed her. It should never have been necessary for Peter to ask it. But she knew that the boy had been worried about his father's past indifference and remembered that specific note he had written and which she had shown Rodney, suggesting that they were being 'cross with each other'. It had troubled him. Well, she had better be thankful that he had kept his word to try and be more fatherly.

She smiled at Peter.

"Maybe Dad's liver was worrying him last hols but now he's feeling better. *I'd* like to have a look at Steve's stamp collection. Let's see it, darling."

The rest of the evening was quite a happy one.

During Christmas, Fran, despite the misery of her bottled-up grief and suspicion that another woman had taken Rod away from her, managed to enjoy herself with Peter. They had spent Christmas Day last year with Rodney's cousins, the Inghams, who had three teenage children – the youngest a girl of Peter's age, and a boy a couple of years older. They all got on quite well, and it was a lovely house for children, with a big garden, on the fringe of Balcombe Forest.

They used also to go over to Eastbourne to spend Boxing Day with Granny. It seemed sad that they wouldn't be taking that journey again. But Peter, nice boy though he was, behaved like most thirteen-year-olds and exhibited no lasting grief for his grandmother. He just said:

"Poor old Gran – rotten luck. Shame her dying . . ." and that ended it. He had a pleasant surprise later on when he learned that she had left him ten pounds to spend as he wanted to, and as his bicycle had been badly damaged in the accident last November, he put the money toward a new and better one.

They stayed in their own home in London this Christmas. Dinner included an elderly uncle on Fran's side, and a recently widowed school-friend with two children who were only too glad to be with Peter. He was rather good with the younger ones. Fran cooked the meal. Everybody helped wash up, and it was quite a gay occasion. Rodney even condescended to put on a paper hat and act the buffoon. Usually he was not good at this sort of fun. But Fran could not fault him over his behaviour this time.

There was one difficult moment – when he came into her room in his dressing-gown, early in the morning, and gave her a small parcel. He said with some geniality:

"Merry Christmas, dear."

Fran didn't take the parcel, so he threw it on the bed. And she didn't give him one.

"I didn't know what to get you," she said, wishing to God that she was not so near to tears. "And as it's your birthday soon, I thought I'd give you one good present for both dates. You might like to choose it, anyhow."

"Okay by me," said Rodney, then: "Aren't you going to open yours?"

She was sitting on the edge of the bed in her dressing-gown. It was not a cold day; it was rather a mild one, but she felt chilled and a bit sick. She was remembering those earrings.

"Well, go on, open it," said Rodney, and seemed mystified by her attitude.

She forced herself to open the parcel. Thank God he hadn't chosen earrings for *her*, she thought cynically. This spray was of more value, obviously, than the aquamarines. Really lovely emeralds, set in gold.

"You've always wanted something like this, haven't you?" she heard Rodney mumble.

She raised brown eyes swimming, glistening, and nodded.

"Thanks awfully, Rod, yes!"

He sat down beside her and put an arm around her – the first time she remembered him doing so since his mother died.

He said:

"For God's sake, don't look so tragic. What have I done? Aren't I being pleasant to my family?"

She swallowed with difficulty.

"Yes, very."

"Then need you look at me as though I'd committed a crime, or don't you like the spray?"

She made an effort to control herself. Then suddenly she broke out:

"I don't understand you. You seem able to turn your feelings on and off just like a tap. I can't, that's all."

He got up. She could see from the changed expression on his face that she had annoyed him and spoilt things.

She went on, wildly:

"Oh, I know you're trying, and that this spray is very valuable and I ought to pretend that I'm quite happy, but I'm not. I'm different from you."

He slid his hands into the pockets of his dressing-gown and look down at her with resentment.

"You, yourself, asked that we should have peace in the house, but perhaps you meant only until the day after Mother's funeral. Now you want to fight again. And on Christmas morning. Not very consistent, are you?"

"No," she said, "not at all. I suppose that I should have thrown my arms around you and kissed you and kissed the emeralds too."

"Now you're being thoroughly beastly."

She beat her right fist into the palm of her left hand, struggling for mastery of her emotions.

"*You know that I know.* You know, but pretend I don't, and I can't pretend, that's all."

He went scarlet. A look of fury puckered his face. He opened his lips, obviously meaning to make some angry remark, but at that precise moment, Peter, also in a dressing-gown, ran into the room. His hair was rough. His eyes were shining. In his hand he held a packet of valuable stamps which had been his father's present.

"Oh, I say, Dad, thanks *awfully*. These are absolutely fab. Steve was talking to me only the other day about that Cape of Good Hope one. He'll be green with envy. Thanks awfully, Dad."

Silence. Rodney turned away from Fran and faced his son, his hands doubling and undoubling at his sides. He forced a light note into his voice.

"Glad you like them, Pete."

Fran looked up. She, too, spoke in a high artificial voice:

"How about you two having your baths? I'm going to get breakfast."

After that, no more was said between husband and wife, neither was the dangerous moment alluded to by either of them. When the festivities were all over and Peter was in bed, Rodney went out.

And that was one of the bitterest moments of Fran's life.

She heard him come back. It was two in the morning. She was convulsed by grief and jealousy. If it hadn't been Christmas night she would have gone into his dressing-room, faced him, and told him that she couldn't go on – that she must have things out with him, but because Pete was in the house she controlled herself.

She did not sleep any more. At half-past five, a bitterly cold Boxing Day, snow-flakes whirled against the window-panes. She went down to the kitchen and made tea for herself.

Her head ached so that she could hardly see out of her eyes. This tension had an effect not only on a woman's nerves but on her whole body, she thought. She had abdominal pains. She felt sick. The sight of her face in the kitchen mirror appalled her. Eyes rimmed with red, lips pale, like her cheeks, and a pinched look which made her appear at least ten years older than she was. If looks meant a lot to a man, she was fast losing hers.

Oh God, she thought, give me the strength to go through this day and the rest of the holidays without a breakdown – for the sake of my son. I won't have him made miserable by his damnable, disloyal father. *I won't.*

When Rodney came down for breakfast, she and Pete had already finished theirs. Fran was sitting with Pete by the sitting-room fire, helping him sort his stamps. A job which obviously gave the boy much satisfaction, so she was satisfied.

Rodney had slept until ten o'clock. When he appeared he looked, she thought cynically, as though he had had a 'night out' – with *that woman.* All night! That woman whose eyes matched the aquamarines. God, how she hated her!

Rodney made an attempt to be jocular, which went down well enough with Peter but had the effect of increasing Fran's sense of misery. When he pretended that all was well to the extent of putting an arm around her shoulders and suggesting that they all went down to the country for a drive, she drew away from him as though his touch repelled her and gave a short cynical laugh.

"Fine idea! Let's all get snowed up on the Sussex Downs. The forecast is frightful and if the snow gets worse we could always pretend we're Eskimos and build ourselves an igloo.'

"Oh, *Mum*!" Peter looked up from his stamps and grimaced. "Come off it."

"Yes, dear, come off it," Rodney echoed the words lightly.

It was too much for Fran. She swung round and hissed at him under her breath.

"You're the one who is going to come off it and very soon. *Very soon . . .*"

He stared at her. She saw that he was quite shocked. She was shocked at herself, and Peter had stared at her. Of course she was usually the quiet long-suffering little woman. He wouldn't understand the way she felt this morning.

She rushed out of the room before her emotions became uncontrollable. She went upstairs to her bedroom. Rodney followed her and shut the door after him.

"What the hell was all that in aid of," he began to question her.

She stormed at him. She told him now exactly what she thought of him.

"It's disgraceful, abominable – leaving this house to go to your girl-friend, staying with her all night, coming back in the early hours then trying to pretend that nothing is wrong and putting an arm around *me* . . ." She gave a laugh that was more of a cry from the depths of her heart. "I don't know how you can be so deceitful – so *awful*!"

"And I don't know what this is all about —" he began, but again she interrupted.

"Oh, yes, you do."

"Look here," said Rodney, his face red and sulky. "You're the one who has been preaching about us not letting the boy know what's happening between us and I've tried to do as you ask and make a good job of it. But look at you this morning – I should think no boy of Pete's age could fail to see there is something very wrong the way you yelled at me and ran out of the room."

Fran started to speak and stopped. She was so tired and tense that all her strength of will, her good sense seemed to leave her. She dissolved into tears, lying across the bed, her face hidden against the pillow.

But even while she wept she remembered her son and looked up at Rodney, sobbing.

"L-lock the d-door – p-please."

He did so. His own heart was sinking, if she but knew it, he thought. He was so used to Fran being sensible and collected, this breakdown unnerved him. For all that Perdita meant to him, he still was unwilling to hurt his wife like this. He knew that she didn't deserve it.

He sat down on the bed and touched her shoulder.

"Don't!" she said with a fresh burst of sobbing, "I hate you. *I hate you!*"

He stood up, feeling in his pocket for a packet of cigarettes.

"Oh God!" he said. "You seem bent on a show-down whether Peter's home or not."

She sat up and faced him, dark hair disordered, her face wet and blotchy.

"You're not going to put me in the wrong. I won't stand for it. I've kept quiet for a long time – right in the background.

I've let you do what you want. Until yesterday, I never let you know that I suspected you. I even let you believe I'd accepted your damned silly story about the aquamarines. *I loved you, Rod.* More than anything in the world. I didn't want to lose you to this girl or any other. But I'm damned if I'm going to be treated like you're treating me nowadays – hearing you creep out of the house like a criminal, and coming back pretending you're a jolly good fellow and all that tripe."

"Fran," he said after a long pause, "I warn you, if you insist on a show-down, you'll make it impossible for me not to have one with you."

She took a corner of the sheet and pressed it against her face.

"And you don't want it. No! You don't want to be put in the wrong. You want to go to *her* when the fancy takes you and then be welcomed back by me as though I still adore you, and trust you, then go visiting her again. Two adoring women at the same time. Ever so satisfactory from *your* point of view. But what about mine?"

Another pause.

"Sneering and accusing me won't help matters," he said at length.

"Nothing will if you want to know."

"Then I might as well pack."

She was silent. Her swollen eyelids blinked. She stared up at him as though stupefied. She whispered:

"So you do want to leave me for someone else?"

Another pause – this one longer than the last. The colour had left Rodney's face. Despite his lie-in, he felt immensely tired and last night he had drunk too much of Perdita's white wine. His tongue and throat were dry. He hadn't even had a cup of tea or coffee yet. He licked his lips and coughed. At last he said:

"Fran, for God's sake, don't force the issue. Not today, anyhow."

"You mean you haven't exactly made up your mind whether you want to leave your wife and son for *her* – or not?"

"I haven't made up my mind about anything. As far as I

know I haven't even admitted that you're right and that there *is* another woman in my life."

"You can't deny it!" Fran said wildly.

"All right, then, there is."

"Who is she?"

"You don't know her."

"Where did you meet her – when?"

"Look," said Rodney in a harsh voice, "I'm not in the mood to be cross-questioned."

"*You're* not in the mood! Anyone would think you are the injured party in this affair. What am I then – the guilty one?"

"For Christ's sake stop being so sarcastic, Fran. I can't take it. Whether I'm guilty or not is not the point. I admit there's somebody else and I know I'm in the wrong and a cad and all that, but this sort of battle won't help us – for the moment, anyhow. Unless, of course, you want me to get out now, in which case I'll quit. But I thought your main concern was for Peter. You seem to have changed your mind."

That completely defeated her. The big guns she had been firing at Rodney had swung round. He had fired a broadside at her. She gave a choking cry and covered her face with her hands. Rodney stood staring at her wretchedly, his cigarette forgotten. His mouth was so dry he couldn't enjoy smoking, anyhow. But one thing he did know – although Perdita had come so incredibly between him and his old love for Fran, Fran was still his wife and the mother of his son, and she looked so utterly pathetic huddled there on the edge of the bed, sobbing. He was moved and shaken.

He sat down beside her. He took one of her hands between his.

"God! you're like ice! . . ."

She did not draw her hand away but went on crying. After a moment he said:

"Fran, I feel all kinds of a bastard, I admit it. You've never done a damned thing to deserve what I've done to you. I admit that, too. But these things happen. They happen to other married couples. You know, we've seen it with friends of our own, and we thought them happy and quite well suited and all that. But someone else comes along in the life of the husband or the wife and well, things change . . . I'm putting the case very badly, but that's the way things are. If you want me to tell you about . . . about *her* . . . I will."

Fran lifted her head and blew her nose.

"I do want you to. I've got to know. It's all been driving me mad because I *don't* know. I'd rather."

"What about Peter —?"

"He needn't know yet. It doesn't necessarily mean that you've got to pack up this moment and go, or anything drastic," Fran said in a small voice, "but I've just *got* to know."

"All right," he said, gave a sigh, stood up, and walked to the window. He watched the snow whirling down – from a darkening sky. Some of the houses opposite were showing lights. It was a Boxing Day that would keep people indoors. He thought of last night and something Perdita had said to him.

"You seem to be getting tied up in knots in yourself, Rod. I give you my word it's no good you making your wife suspicious and upsetting the whole apple-cart, because no matter what you say, I don't intend to have a permanent affair with you. Neither am I going to be involved in a divorce. I warn you, darling. Much as I adore sleeping with you, I just warn you, that's all. This isn't for keeps. It never has been."

That's what she had said and not for the first time. Possibly it was that ice-cold attitude of hers, that apparent lack of heart, that was three-quarters of her attraction for him. But he had forgotten Fran last night, as usual, *and* the warning. With Perdita lying in his arms he was able to forget anything except his insane passion for her.

Now, forced into this scene by Fran he felt uncertain and ill at ease. Above all, he was genuinely remorseful because he had brought Fran down so low. This sobbing, hysterical creature was far removed from the old Fran with her gaiety, her spirit, her courage, her natural dignity.

However, if she insisted on hearing the truth, she had better hear it.

He began to tell her about Perdita.

13

"Come in, come in," said Peter's Housemaster.

Mr. Inholm did not really want to be disturbed. He was in the process of writing a difficult letter to the widowed mother of a boy who had had an exceedingly bad report last term. The said mother was quite convinced that her son was an angel and that he, with the Headmaster, was responsible for the report and just did not understand. She had written a somewhat angry letter to him.

He looked up from the blotter and his frown changed to a smile as he saw the tall thin boy with the unruly thatch of dark hair come into the room.

"Hello, Grifford. What can I do for you?"

Peter Grifford avoided his Housemaster's eye. He moved rather nervously nearer the desk. He was, as a rule, at ease with this man who was a kindly and tolerant person, but at this particular moment, Peter was suffering from acute anxiety. He had been eating, sleeping, and working badly.

Mr. Inholm had a perceptive eye and was quick to notice the expression on Grifford's face. As a rule, he was one of the brightest and nicest pupils here and he got on well with the Staff.

"Sit down and relax," said Mr. Inholm. "What's worrying you?"

Grifford cleared his throat but refused to sit down.

"I'd rather stand, thank you, sir."

The Housemaster took up his pipe and put the stem between his teeth.

"Just as you like."

Peter cleared his throat.

"You may think me rather silly, sir."

"Well, don't let's start on that basis. Let's take it for granted that I find you fairly intelligent."

Peter cleared his throat.

"It's about my home, sir."

"What about it, Grifford?"

"My – my parents, sir."

The Housemaster sighed. Not another of those! He had had rather too many unhappy boys lately, disturbed because of disruption between their parents. Damn it, why couldn't young couples today carry out the promises they made to each other at the altar? And the Griffords were not all that young, anyhow. This lad was in his early teens. Quickly the Housemaster searched his memory. He could summon up a fair picture of Grifford's parents as he had seen them at the end of the winter term.

"You needn't feel awkward, Grifford," at last Mr. Inholm remarked. "I shall understand, and respect your confidence."

Peter twisted and untwisted his fingers behind his back. He, himself, hadn't far to search his own memory. He had a very clear vision of a certain day when he had approached the Head of his Prep. School about young Butler, whose parents had been about to get a divorce. And he remembered some of the things the Head had said, and how decent he had been.

Peter had been back here for well over a week now and chewed over and over again in his mind the idea of consulting his Housemaster about his own difficulties. So here he was. But it wasn't easy to speak his mind. Nevertheless the Housemaster's geniality encouraged him. He said:

"Well, you see sir, it's like this. I'm terribly afraid my parents are going to separate."

Mr. Inholm sighed. Here we go again, he thought. These matrimonial disputes always reacted poorly on the kids. And for Grifford it was at an especially bad time – only just beginning his education at Public School; an adolescent who needed both the affection and sympathy his mother could give, and the friendship and example he ought to get from his father.

"I'm sorry to hear this, Grifford, but I'm afraid if it's really so, there isn't much I can do. But are you sure it isn't only a temporary – er – dispute between your parents? Perhaps they just want to get away from one another for a time, and so on. But they'll come back and it will all be all right, eh?"

Peter reddened, shyness and misery enveloping him.

"Please, sir, I think it's worse than that. I'm afraid I cheated. I mean, on Boxing Day I heard my parents quarrelling and I listened outside the door. I know I oughtn't to have done, but I did."

The Housemaster gave him a faint smile.

"We've all been guilty of that at some time in our lives, Grifford. Sometimes it's too much of a temptation, isn't it?"

Peter shifted from one foot to the other.

"Yes, sir."

"And you heard your parents quarrelling?"

"Yes, sir, and my mother crying and all that, and then they both shouted and I heard my father admit that he – well – that he was seeing another woman and all that, and my mother cried again and said something about my father, but I didn't understand it all and I buzzed off after a bit. Then I heard them on at each other later in the hols, and just before I came back to school it was worse and I know something's up. I've never seen my mother so upset."

"I'm very sorry indeed, Grifford. You have all my sympathy. But it may not be as bad as you imagine.'

"I'm afraid it is, sir. I heard my mother tell Dad that she had never known him be so nice to me – like offering to take me out and all that, and she said she was sure it was because he was trying to get me on his side."

"Oh dear!" said Mr. Inholm uneasily.

"I know they mean to get a divorce. I know they've only been waiting for me to come back to school to fix it up."

"Come, come, I'm sure you're making it all rather more serious than it is."

But young Grifford stuck to his story and at the end of it Mr Inholm, feeling exceedingly uneasy, said:

"What exactly do you want me to do, Grifford? I'll help you if I can, of course, but I can't really interfere in so personal a matter between your parents."

But Peter Grifford was remembering something else his recent Headmaster had said about his friend Butler . . . *if* his parents were always fighting and he was always hearing rows, he might be happier if they separated.

He also remembered what Butler had said about that.

Now, Peter quoted Butler's very words:

"Please, sir, I'd rather hear the rows than lose either of them. I wish you could tell them so. You see, sir, one of my friends had the same thing happen at my Prep. School, and he said he'd rather put up with hearing all the quarrelling than have his parents divorced, and I feel the same way."

The Housemaster locked his fingers behind his back and without facing Grifford, said:

"I'll try to have a word with your parents. I'll do what I can."

"Thank you, sir."

When the Housemaster turned round the boy had gone.

"Damn," said Martin Inholm softly to himself. "*Damn!*"

But being a man of his word and on Grifford's side, he carried out his promise.

He wrote a letter to Rodney Grifford and asked him if he and his wife could possibly come down to the school during this weekend to see him. He added that he would rather they did not refer to the visit, should they be writing to their son.

14

"Now you see what you've done to your son," said Fran bitterly and not very tactfully, during the drive back from Peter's school that bleak January Sunday afternoon.

Rodney, who hadn't had as many drinks as he needed, on account of the Breathalyser, and who was in a state of nerves anyhow, snapped back:

"That's right – put all the blame on me."

"I'd like to ask why *I* should be blamed, except that I was stupid enough to be goaded into quarrelling with you, and Pete heard us. But I've never been unfaithful to you and up to a short time ago I adored the ground you walked on. You've never really loved me – that's the crux of the matter and you've never been as interested in Peter as most fathers are in their sons. So I *do* blame you."

"Splendid," said Rodney furiously, and pulled the car up with a jerk.

They were on a lay-by. The weekend traffic was not heavy because it had been drizzling since early morning. It was growing dark. By invitation of Peter's Housemaster they had gone down to the school after lunch. It hadn't been a very happy lunch either. Rodney had suddenly, openly announced his intention of leaving Fran.

"I don't want a divorce," he had said, "and if you're generous enough to be broadminded and let me get this thing out of my system, it might all come right in the end. But you keep on and on about this girl and if it's a divorce you want – we'll have to have one."

"I don't know," she answered, "but I told you only the other day that I didn't want Peter disturbed at his age."

"Well, I can't stand you always being either in tears or furious with me, and accusing me of something. I just can't take it any more."

"And what about what *I'm* required to take – all this humiliation, and misery? You don't seem to realise what you've done to me."

"Yes, I do," he had told her gloomily, "and that is why I really can't stand it. No man likes to be made to feel such a bastard. I'd rather end it all and be out of it."

Then, Fran, with little of her old patience and gentle tolerance left, screamed:

"And what *are* you, if you're not a bastard? Just tell me. Are you a hero for picking up this beautiful, gorgeous girl who works on computers, and spending most of your spare time with her instead of with your wife?"

"It's no use going over the same thing," he sighed. "It won't get us anywhere."

Then Fran, more controlled, said:

"Very well, Rodney. Do as you please, but I won't divorce you. And I won't let this hurt Peter. I'd rather put up with anything than that."

Sunk in misery, she slumped back in the car while Rodney lit a cigarette and smoked in silence. She was remembering that scene at lunch. And it all seemed much worse now they had been warned that *Peter knew*. The humiliation had been complete, when Martin Inholm had told them as kindly and nicely as he could, that the boy knew that his parents were considering divorce, and that he had said that he would rather put up with all the quarrelling he heard than lose either one of them.

To her, such love and loyalty seemed infinitely pathetic. She had had to dig her finger-nails into the palms of her hands in order not to break down and sob in front of Mr. Inholm. How Rodney took it, she dared not imagine, but she was sure he felt both shame and distress. He had got up from his chair and walked to the window rather than let the Housemaster see his face. The latter had been extremely tactful and friendly.

"These things happen – I'm afraid all too often, but I always tell parents who are in such a position, if I am privileged to be in their confidence, to try and remember both of them *are*, indeed, needed by their children. To Peter, Mr. Grifford, you, his father, must always be the figurehead and backbone of the family. That's natural."

"Thanks awfully for seeing us," Rod had said as they left. "We will do all we can to avoid hurting the boy."

This had given Fran some hope, but here they were, she thought wretchedly, at each other's throats again. What *were* they going to do?

Rodney stared through the wet windscreen at the lights gleaming on the tarmac and at the dazzle of lights from the oncoming cars on the other side of the carriage-way.

He felt deflated this evening. His mad infatuation for Perdita could not totally destroy his inborn sense of propriety; of duty and honour toward his wife and son. The conversation with Mr. Inholm had come as something of a shock to him. As long as the Perdita affair was kept secret – and none of their friends knew about it – he had felt he could cope. But to hear Peter's Housemaster on the subject had been scarcely pleasant. Not that the man had said anything that could offend. But when they had come away from the school without seeing Peter, Rodney had felt a sudden unaccustomed sensation of loss. Almost as though he was disappointed because he had driven all that way down to the school and not caught a glimpse of the boy. Fran was undoubtedly feeling the same, if not worse.

But what if he decided to leave home and wouldn't be there when Peter came back for the Easter holidays? Where would he, Rodney, be, anyhow? Perdita had informed him categorically that she was leaving for New York to take up her job at the beginning of February. She had also told him, not for the first time, that she did not want him to follow her.

"Your job's in London and you can't afford to leave it. And what's more, much as I like living with you now in the way we do, I don't want you to break up your home because of me. I keep telling you so."

When he had suggested that they might both be happier if he left home and took a flat of his own, even though Fran did not want a divorce, Perdita had said "*No*".

"Wait till I've gone to America. Maybe you'll be able to get me out of your system then."

"That," he said with savage passion, "is out of the question."

He could hardly bear to be away from her for a day or night. It was freedom he wanted. Freedom to go where he wanted when he wanted, and not to be constantly beholden to his wife.

But this evening, after the discussion with Peter's Housemaster, fresh doubts and difficulties presented themselves to Rodney.

He hadn't confided his troubles in his old friend George; George who was responsible for introducing him to Perdita. No one could blame him for *that*. Feeling particularly worried and uneasy one day last week, he had taken Ted Lock out for lunch – Ted whom he had known since their Cambridge days, and told him about the affair. He did not expect sympathy and did not get it, Ted was a man of high integrity and devoted to his wife, Harriet. In a friendly way he said a few harsh words that Rodney swallowed, well aware that he had earned them.

"You're a bloody fool, Rod. A lot of men get these crazes and I don't deny that I find these young girls very exciting today, but I wouldn't exchange my old Harriet for a single one of 'em. You've got a damned good little wife in Fran. *And* you've got a son, something Harriet and I would have given a lot for. You'd only spend a few hectic months with this so-called goddess – then what? You'd regret it, and you would have spoiled Fran's and Peter's lives – and your own."

Ted, as Rodney expected, then lectured him on the subject of Peter.

"Don't do it, particularly for the boy's sake, Rodney. Have your fling, then say goodbye to the girl, for God's sake."

The confession hadn't really done much good. Rodney already knew all the things Ted said. His reproaches and warnings could not cool the fever that rose in Rodney every time he saw Perdita.

He began to feel as though he were under a hypnotic spell. He wished to God he'd never met Perdita. Tonight, sitting in the car with Fran, he emerged from a morass of self-pity and futile longing for this girl, and tried to consider the whole thing from Fran's side, alone.

What would she do if he quit? Suddenly, stupidly, Rod asked her about it.

"Fran, we haven't been getting on very well for a long time. Wouldn't you be happier if I wasn't around the place?"

She was silent for a few seconds, grabbed the packet of cigarettes on the seat between them, lit one, and threw the match out of the window which she quickly wound up again because it was a raw night.

Life, the home, without Rod? Freedom to do as she wished when Peter was at school? She might even take a job of sorts. She was well aware that she wouldn't get so many invitations without a husband. Lone women are never so popular. Everybody would be sorry for her at first and down on Rodney, then life would have to go on and she'd be forced to make a new existence for herself. Besides all this, no matter how badly she felt she had been treated by Rodney, she could not quite tear the roots of her old love for him out of her heart. She was the faithful kind, she told herself with bitterness. More than he deserved. She had never looked to right or left since they married.

Of course there was her father, in Johannesburg. She had always been very fond of him and regretted that he had married a South African girl and settled out there with her. He had often asked her and Rod to go out and stay but they had never got down to it. She could take a trip to South Africa and stay with Daddy. She was still a youngish woman and had kept her figure. No doubt some man might find her attractive and eventually fill the gap in her life. Yet the mere idea of putting anybody in Rodney's place filled her with horror. She just couldn't do it. She wasn't going to divorce him now, anyhow. She *wasn't*. She wouldn't hang on to him interminably, like some injured wives, out of sheer malice. He could go free once Peter was through his schooling – but not until then. She told Rod so now, not for the first time.

"And it's no good asking me whether I'd be happy or unhappy," she said. "I won't contemplate an immediate divorce."

"That's foolish of you. You ought to be ready and willing."

"Why? You can't be in such a hurry or you'd have left me before this. Isn't *she* sure she wants *you*? Is that it?"

He felt his face burn in the darkness.

He had never told Fran the whole truth about Perdita. Now she suddenly began to question him.

"What is she like, this wonderful girl who seems to have got right under your skin? *Is* she so wonderful?"

"Obviously I think so."

Fran bit her lips but continued with a touch of masochism to ask him about Perdita. He answered briefly. For the first time Fran began to picture the girl with her extraordinary mentality. And her physical beauty. Finally Fran laughed unpleasantly.

"Gracious, goodness me! You did hit the moon. Poor little

me. I must seem pretty insignificant beside such a unique creature."

"You don't – not in the least," he said with sincerity, and a sudden loathing of himself. "You're absolutely sweet, Fran, and always have been."

"That's absurd! From all you've said and done lately, you've made it quite plain that you don't find me in the least attractive any more."

"Fran, that's not true."

"Oh, don't start that business about you only wish I had been your sister or something, so we could have been friends, and all that. The plain truth is you don't want to go to bed with me any more —"

Fran broke off and covered her face with her hands. A gasping sob broke from her throat. Rodney groaned and tried to put a comforting arm around her, but she shook herself free.

"Don't, please!"

"Fran, I swear that I don't find you unattractive. I'm still terribly fond of you. We've been through so much together. I never forget how good you were to my mother. It's just something – something I can't explain, but this girl has bewitched me."

Fran went on sobbing.

"What am I expected to do? Wait till the witch departs, then try to pick up any bits she cares to leave behind?"

"You're very bitter," said Rodney. "Of course, I'm not surprised."

She choked, blew her nose violently, and stopped crying. She had not meant to break down in front of Rodney. Where was her pride, she asked herself, tragically.

"Hadn't we better go home?" She whispered the question.

"I suppose so."

In unhappy silence they continued the journey.

Back in her home, Fran did not bother even to look at her face or straighten her hair. She took off her coat and scarf and went straight to the kitchen. It was long past eight. She felt sick, but no doubt Rodney would want his usual cold Sunday supper. She started to unwrap some ham she had bought yesterday. Then she wrapped it up again and marched into the sitting-room where Rodney was standing in front of the electric fire, lighting a cigar. It struck her in that moment that he looked rather elderly and careworn. Perdita, the witch, wasn't doing him much good, she thought. She said:

"Do I prepare a meal or are you going out to see your girl-friend?"

"No, I'm not," he said sullenly.

"There's just one more thing I'd like to ask you, Rod. What sort of a girl is she that she has no compunction in coming between husband and wife like this?"

"She didn't come between us."

"Of course she did. Or did you lose interest in me ages ago? Have I been deaf and blind all these years?"

"Not at all. I repeat what I said in the car, Fran. I think you're very sweet and always will think so. Both of us have been unhappy and our nerves have been on edge and with all this fighting, we've probably said things that neither of us has meant. But Perdita did *not* come between us. She's sixteen years younger than I am. I'm the one to blame."

"Her youth doesn't seem to have stopped her from acquiring somebody else's husband. She must be a very strong character."

Rodney frowned. He didn't like discussing his mistress with his wife. It didn't seem decent. But Fran wanted to know more about Perdita so he carried on.

"Yes, she has a powerful personality, I agree. But there's one thing I assure you – she has never asked me to leave you for her. On the contrary, she's off to America at any moment to do a job."

Fran saw a patch of moisture on the polished surface of the pie-crust table by the fireplace. Obviously some water had fallen from one of the white chrysanthemums. Habit made her open a top drawer in a bureau in which she kept a duster, and rub the wet stain away. Then she turned and looked at her husband.

"Are you contemplating leaving me and the Stock Exchange *and* your son in order to pursue this paragon to the States?"

He wanted to answer "*No*", and so put an end to Fran's anxiety and his own sense of impending disaster. Yet he could not. The word stuck in his throat. He thought of Perdita – that tall lovely golden girl in his arms; her beautiful fresh pink lips curled with sudden laughter, those ice-blue eyes mocking him at one moment and darkening with desire for him the next. Oh, damn, *damn* Perdita! What in God's name was he to do?

"Well," said Fran. "Answer me."

He looked at her white face, tired and plain tonight without the usual make-up, and her dark untidy hair. He had never seen Fran untidy before. She was usually so meticulous about her appearance. He could see that she was suffering and it didn't make things any better to know what he was doing to her.

At last he said:

"Perdita doesn't want me to go to America with her. Of course I can't guarantee I might not wish to visit her later on. I've got to be honest about things now, haven't I, Fran? I don't want to hurt you, but I can't go on lying."

She doubled her hands into two tight little fists.

"I prefer honesty."

"But," he added, "there isn't any question of us divorcing if you don't want to chuck me out."

There was silence between them. Once again Fran rubbed the table with the duster. She couldn't see what she was doing. Her eyes were hot with tears. She felt completely broken all of a sudden. But there was somebody to pick up the pieces. Her son. And there were the Easter holidays to look forward to. In a muffled voice, she said:

"You don't give me much choice. I presume if I say I won't stand for you going to see that girl, you'll leave home."

"It sounds ghastly and horribly selfish of me —" he began.

She turned on him, eyes blazing with tears.

"I don't say you're horrible, but I do think you're terribly weak. I never used to think so but I do now, and I can't respect you any more. I know there are lots of unfaithful husbands. I've had two women friends who've found their husbands out. I just never thought I'd be one of them. Oh, you're all so selfish and sensual, *all* you men."

Rodney tugged at his collar.

"I'm sorry."

"I remember a couple we both knew, Bob and Anita Crieff. Do you remember? He suddenly went crazy about a young girl, then Anita forgave him and they sorted it all out but —"

"I'm not asking you to forgive me," Rodney interrupted. "I don't deserve it."

"But Peter deserves some consideration. Yes – I say the same old thing, over and over again, Rod. I won't let you hurt him while he's still so young. He knows we've been fighting and he doesn't want us to have a divorce like the Butlers did. He still sees the Butler boy who was at his other school. He's often told me how young Butler loathes the split, having to go first to one parent's house, then to the other's. Peter must not be disturbed like that. So please stay with us – and if you must – go on seeing your girl-friend. I won't ask questions. Just don't tell me when and where you're going. But for Peter's sake – and your own reputation, let's try to behave well in public. Don't cancel every arrangement I make for us to go out to friends or entertain them. Don't start a scandal. And – and —"

Fran broke off and ran out of the room. Rodney heard her go up the stairs and slam her bedroom door.

"Oh God," he said aloud. "*God*, what a mess!"

He turned, leaned an arm against the mantelpiece and put his forehead against it.

15

DURING the month that followed, Fran had not the slightest idea what was going on in her husband's mind. That he continued to see the girl Perdita she was sure, although he had obviously been shaken up by the visit to the Housemaster, as well as the discussion he had had with Fran on the subject of Perdita, and was curtailing his 'evenings out'.

They went to their dinner parties and the usual Bridge with the Locks.

They attended a Charity ball together. Fran was on the committee. It was an annual event.

In this case, Rodney insisted on giving Fran a generous cheque to buy herself a new dress for the occasion. At first she refused but he insisted.

"There's no need to be so proud that you can't let me buy you a new dress."

In the end she took the money and bought the dress.

She wondered, with a touch of remorse, why she had been so sure of her husband and his affection for her, so certain that he would never leave her for another woman, and feared she had not taken as much care of herself as she should have done. She had been stupid, perhaps, to be certain she would never have a rival. But even now that she knew, it was not easy for a woman nearing forty to line herself up beside a young beautiful girl. But with some of her old spirit, Fran set out to compete.

When Rodney first saw his wife on the night of the Ball she was a new and much more attractive Fran. She felt a thrill of pleasure as she saw the look of admiration in his eyes, a look she had not seen for a long time.

"I say – terrific!" he said warmly.

The long evening dress was of pale gold satin, tight about hips and waist, the off-the-shoulder corsage encrusted with seed-pearls and diamanté.

She wore pearl and diamond earrings, and her hair had been beautifully cut and brushed. She had spent an hour or two in a Beauty Salon where she had a special facial and make-up. The girl had insisted on giving her more eye-shadow than she normally used – mauve and gold. It made Fran's soft brown eyes look enormous and dramatic.

She drew on long gold gloves and picked up her bag.

"Shall we go?" she said, and felt suddenly embarrassed by Rodney's stare.

He said:

"You look stunning, Fran. I'd like to kiss you but I know you won't want me to."

"Oh, don't let's get all sentimental," she snapped, in order to gulp back her sudden emotion. She couldn't afford to be sentimental with this husband of hers. She had been too badly hurt.

He was very nice for the rest of the evening and danced with her more often than he need. But once they were home again he went straight to his bedroom and she to hers. He said:

"Good-night, Fran. It's been a great success and I'm sure the Committee ought to be very grateful to you for all you did."

After she had said good-night and closed her door, Fran took off her jewellery and the beautiful dress, lay down on her bed and put her flushed face against the pillow. She felt suddenly drained of vitality. Her feet ached. She had danced the whole night. And she had been horrified to find that none of her other partners mattered. She had enjoyed dancing only with her husband. So she was still in love with him, she thought unhappily. That seemed so awful. For if he still found this girl attractive, and still wanted her, he would eventually go to her. She, his wife, could do nothing now but mark time.

The name 'Perdita' was never now mentioned between them but Fran was perfectly well aware that he saw her. She always knew . . .

And, of course, at the end of February there came the usual 'business' trip to Paris. She used to believe absolutely that he went over to see his Parisian client but now although she did not ask, she felt certain it would also mean a liaison with his girl-friend.

After he had packed and gone, Fran felt so miserable and deflated, she began to wonder if this situation was worth while even for Peter. She began to wonder too, if she would go on playing the part that Anita Crieff had played – and she remembered Anita telling her what she had been through in order to keep Bob. It was too humiliating.

In a sudden wild mood, Fran sat down and scribbled a letter to her father.

"Rodney and I are no longer happy. As he has found someone else, I am going to sue for divorce. I want to come out to you. I hope Sally won't mind. It'll only be for a month or so and we can talk things over, and I'll decide whether to keep Peter in England or bring him out to S. Africa to make a new life there . . ."

She stopped writing and opened the drawer of her bureau in order to get some fresh writing paper. She saw, lying on the top, the last letter that had come from Peter on Monday. He always wrote home during the weekends. She sat back and re-read it:

"Dad's been very decent about writing lately and I always get a letter from him every week now. He says he's going to talk to you about buying a boat for us and going down to Chichester to launch it, and we could spend some of the Easter hols and summer down there. Absolutely fab."

Fran clenched her hands over this letter and closed her eyes. This was a form of self-imposed torture, she thought, this endeavour to keep the family together. Here was Rodney behaving more like a proper father to the boy than he had ever done before, and here was Peter writing with affection and pleasure about 'Dad'.

What would his feelings be if she were to write and prick the bubble of his enthusiasm? If she told him that, after all, his parents couldn't get on and there was to be a divorce?

Suddenly Fran tore up the letter she had started to write to her father. The tears dripped down her cheeks. She wiped them away and told herself to try not to be idiotic. It was she who had originally manoeuvred the plan of keeping the family together while Peter was a schoolboy. What right had she to turn her back on all she had said, or to lecture Rodney. She had just *got* to carry on.

But supposing *Rodney* weakened. Supposing *that girl* began to be more demanding and wanted him soon – body and soul? Supposing Rodney decided that he couldn't live apart from her, and that his occasional visits were not enough?

There was only one thing to do, Fran thought, if one sank into this state, one must get down to a very ordinary, insignificant task.

She went into her husband's dressing-room and opened the two top drawers of the big bow-fronted chest-of-drawers.

For a long time she had promised herself that she would look through Rodney's socks and do some mending, and send some of his ties to the cleaners. A wifely duty she had not bothered about lately. There had been so many other things on her mind.

The tears continued to drip down her cheeks as she unrolled the socks and examined them, laid some aside, and put the others back in the drawer. She sniffed as she worked, and rubbed her wet face with the back of her hand.

As she finished sorting, she suddenly remembered a night when she had noticed a button missing from Rodney's pyjama jacket. It was his nice dark blue silk pair with white braid which she had bought him it seemed ages ago, before all this nightmare had descended on her.

He kept his pyjamas in the bottom drawer. She opened it and started to look through a rather untidy collection of undergarments, shirts and pullovers. It seemed to her high time she put it all in order. It was a sign of the times. Rodney used to be so very orderly and careful with his things. Now he was very careless. Funny how an affair like this could change a man's habits in even so slight a way.

Lifting the things out one by one, Fran came across a large envelope with cardboard backing. It was marked – PHOTOGRAPH.

Overcome by curiosity she drew out the contents. Then she sat very still, looking with anguished eyes at the face of her little daughter, Miranda.

It was the photograph that used to stand on this bureau. Rodney's treasure. He had put it away after the child's death. He would not even allow her to have one out where he could see it. Indeed, she felt this morning, as though she was looking at a stranger; as though Miranda had never existed. The anguish in her heart was almost insupportable. How beautiful Miranda had been! The photograph in colour, showed the little girl's exquisite colouring. Her bright fair curls and amazingly blue eyes. The Grifford eyes.

With trembling fingers Fran began to push the photograph back into the envelope. It gave her too much pain to look at it. The photograph seemed to jam and as she put in her hand she came across a second one. This time she stared with profound astonishment. Also in colour, it was of someone she did not know. The strikingly beautiful head and shoulders of a girl whom Fran imagined must be in her late teens or early twenties. She was wearing a canary-yellow, polo-necked sweater. Long amber hair cascaded on either side of the classic face.

For a stricken moment, Fran stared into the girl's eyes – eyes as blue as aquamarines – *as blue as Miranda's.*

Then the truth exploded in her mind. *Of course . . . this was Perdita.* This was the girl Rodney was so madly in love with . . . Aquamarine eyes . . . Fran felt an hysterical laugh rising in her throat. Of course. He had bought those aquamarine earrings for *her*.

Fran could not stop staring. The girl's face drew her attention like a powerful magnet she was unable to resist.

This was Perdita and oh! Perdita was gorgeous. Oh, poor, poor Rodney! What man wouldn't find her gorgeous, more especially if she had a liking for him?

Then the other aspect smote Fran again. The strange likeness between this girl and Miranda. It was undeniable. And maybe this was it; Rodney was entranced and intrigued because Perdita was an adult edition of their little daughter – she was Miranda as she might have looked had she lived.

But, of course, none of that excused him. Fran let the two photographs fall on her lap, pressed her hands against her face, and rocked herself to and fro.

"God!" she said. "God! I can't bear it!"

How dared he put those two photographs together in one

envelope in his drawer. Their innocent child and that girl whom he had made his mistress. It was going too far.

Sobbing aloud she made a movement as though to tear Perdita's photograph in half. Then she heard a voice in the doorway.

"Don't, Fran. *Please don't.*"

She looked up through her blurred eyes and saw Rodney standing in the room. He was still wearing his dark blue overcoat. It must be snowing. She noticed the white flakes on his shoulders, on his thick fair hair. He looked ill – ghastly.

"What on earth is it? Are you all right?" she asked and slowly and painfully got to her feet, still holding the two photographs.

Rodney took them from her.

"I thought you were in Paris," Fran added dully.

"I didn't go," he said.

"Why not?"

"I had an urgent message just before I left the office for the Airport. They sent for me from the hospital. She was in an accident."

Fran stared:

"Who was?"

"Perdita," he said in quite a calm, detached sort of voice.

"*Perdita,*" Fran repeated.

"Yes. She was on her way to meet me at Heathrow. You might as well know. We were going to Paris together. It was for the last time, because she had had her marching orders to America. She was leaving England next week. I was going to lose her, anyhow."

"What do you mean?"

"I mean I shall never see her again, Fran. By the time I got to the hospital she was in a bad way. She only just recognised me. She's dying, they say."

Fran stood quite still and silent. Of course she realised that she could have said all kinds of things such as '*Well, that ends that*' or '*I'm afraid I don't care*' or '*What do you expect me to do – burst into tears?*'

But she felt, curiously, as though this girl, Perdita, had never played a part in her life. She exclaimed:

"Oh, Rod, how absolutely *ghastly*!"

He sat down and fumbled in his pocket for a packet of cigarettes, found it empty and let it drop on the floor. Fran went to a drawer. She knew he kept a store there. She pulled out a box, lit one of the cigarettes, and handed it to him.

"Thanks," he said without looking at her.

"How did it happen?"

"She had just left this place in the City where she worked on computers. An American friend of hers, Robert they call him . . . he got her the job in America . . . called for her in his car. It appears that they . . . well, Robert jumped the lights just as they reached Westminster Bridge. It was a head-on crash into a lorry swinging around in front of them. Robert's car had a left-hand drive. He was killed outright and Perdita was terribly injured."

"Oh, how ghastly." Fran repeated the words in a whisper.

Now she looked down at the big photograph of the girl with the lovely face that reminded her of her dead child. Rodney looked at it, too. He shook his head.

"No – her face wasn't hurt. But her body was crushed. They said she was conscious when they pulled her out and nobody knows why she's lived so long. It was because she was so strong . . ."

Fran heard the crack in his voice and saw such naked pain in his eyes that she could hardly bear it. Her own injured pride and misery seemed of little importance beside this major tragedy – his and Perdita's. Terrible that such a lovely young girl should die. Some people would call it retribution. She had been on her way to meet another woman's husband and fly to Paris with him. But who was she, Fran, to judge? She had never been in love with anybody but Rod. She had never been tempted.

She laid the photograph down on the bed, walked up to her husband, and put her arms around him.

"I'm terribly sorry," she said. "*Terribly* sorry."

The face he raised to her was ugly with grief – with rage because Perdita must die – was probably dead by now. He said:

"Why the hell should *you* be sorry after all I've done to you?"

"But I *am* —" She began to protest.

He broke away from her arms and stood up.

"For God's sake, don't be. I can't stand it."

She could understand that. She was not even offended because he had rejected her.

"If you want to go back to the hospital and stay with Perdita, please do," she said.

He said nothing. He seemed stunned. Fran went on:

"Has she any relatives or close friends in London?"

"Nobody, Fran. Absolutely nobody. Only an aunt in New Zealand, and I don't think she'd come over as Perdita said she had had an operation recently and is in poor health. I saw the doctor in charge of Perdita and he said it's just a question of hours. I don't know the medical details. I don't suppose it matters."

"You'd better go back to the hospital," said Fran.

Now he took the cigarette from his lips and stared down at her. He felt half crazy with shock and grief but realised how generously Fran was behaving.

"Oh, Fran," he said, "you're really so good about this. I do thank you. I —" He broke off and shrugged his shoulders in a hopeless sort of way.

"Go back to the hospital," she said for the third time. "I don't mind. I promise you I don't."

He sat down again heavily and put a hand over his eyes.

"I feel a bit odd . . ."

"You want a nip of brandy."

She went downstairs, fetched the brandy, and made him drink it. Afterwards he put the empty glass down, drew a long breath, and wiped his lips.

"Thanks. I'm all right now."

"It was the shock," she said.

She saw his red-rimmed eyes travel to the photograph on the

bed. She could read his mind like a book. She had often been able to do that.

"Don't worry," she said, "I won't tear it up. Poor Rod! It's all you'll have left."

"I suppose you'll say I don't deserve any more."

"I haven't said so, have I?"

"No, you've been angelic. Oh God, what a bloody mess it all is!"

"Well, let's keep a sense of proportion and remember that the girl is dying and that she might like to see you again," said Fran, and walked to the window and stared out.

For all her *sang-froid* she was beginning to feel a trifle sick. She had never seen Rod look so down and out. At least, not since the tragedy of their little daughter's death. She pitied him. It seemed that Rod was cut out to lose those he loved the most. In this moment Fran experienced a dreadful sense of loneliness. She couldn't include herself among those whom Rod loved – no – not any more. The knife of her own bitterness and pain seemed to be turning in her vitals. It seemed too, that her vocal cords were cut so that she couldn't even cry out and say: "*What about my pain and loss? I loved you. You were mine. And I was yours until she took you away.*"

She felt Rod's hand on her shoulder.

"You've been remarkably generous. I won't forget it. But I'd like to take advantage of it and get back to the hospital now."

"You should never have left."

"They wouldn't let me sit by her and I had to tell you that I wouldn't be going to Paris."

"You could have 'phoned," said Fran stonily, without turning to look at him.

"I suppose so. But I just came home," he said in a hopeless sort of voice.

She swung round.

"Why don't you *go*?"

"I don't know. I want to yet I don't."

"Would you like me to go with you?"

Now he opened his eyes wide.

"Isn't that carrying things a bit too far?"

"Perhaps, but it doesn't seem to matter. If I can be of any help, I'll willingly come along. I don't need to stay there but I'd like to tell her that I didn't really mind about you and her and that I don't want her to die feeling bad about me."

"Oh, my God!" said Rodney under his breath.

"I assure you," said Fran hastily, "that I'm not planning a big 'I forgive you' scene. I'm just taking it for granted that she might have some conscience about me so I want her to feel I don't mind."

"But you do," he said stupidly. "I know you do and that's what I most dislike. I swear I didn't want to hurt you."

"You seem to hurt everybody without realising you're doing it," she said with sudden rage. "Do stop talking and let's go to the hospital. Perdita might have been your daughter, mightn't she? That's what started it all, isn't it, that father-daughter image? Well – you ought to be with her now."

He was defeated by such perception. He hadn't dreamed Fran knew all this. She was in this hour a Fran he had never known. It wasn't any good lying to her any more.

"All right," he said, "that's what started it. When I first saw Perdita with those eyes and that hair – I found her curiously like Miranda. I thought our daughter might well have grown up to look a bit like Perdita, only smaller."

The knife turned in Fran's heart again. She walked to the door.

"All the more reason that we should do what we can for Perdita. She has nobody else. You've been living with her so you're in a way responsible. After all, she was just about to go to Paris with you."

"Okay, I'm responsible," said Rodney grimly.

"I'll get my coat," said Fran. "Have you got the car?"

"No."

" 'Phone for a taxi. It's snowing quite hard."

"I'll try the rank," he said. "Fran . . ." he called out to her.

"What?"

"You don't have to come."

"That's neither here nor there. Do you want me to?"

"Yes, I do," he said, and for the first time tears burned his eyes.

16

If Fran had felt a curious detachment when Rodney told her about Perdita's accident, she felt it again when finally she sat beside the girl's bed and stared at her.

The doctor in 'Casualty' spoke to the Griffords before they came into the Ward. He told them that Miss Shaw was still alive and that considering how badly hurt she was, she was holding on astonishingly well. She certainly didn't seem to want to die, he said.

"Is there any chance of her surviving?" Rodney had asked.

"I doubt it. Such a fabulous girl, too," was the young doctor's regretful reply.

Now Fran examined that extraordinarily beautiful face. Untouched, as Rodney had said, cheeks and lips very pale; no colour except in the gold of the long strands of hair. A nurse had brushed it. It fell on either side of that classic face like a gilded frame.

Of course, Fran thought, she really *isn't* like Miranda who had been such a baby when she died, with a small rosy mouth and button nose. Yet the likeness was there; in the width of the forehead, the shape of the brows, and the cleft in the chin. *And* the hair.

So far, after sitting here with Rodney for half an hour, Perdita had not opened her eyes. The long lashes were not lifted. Fran could see how tall Perdita must be. Her body was outlined under the red hospital blanket. Poor girl, thought Fran; driving to the Airport to meet her lover. All set for a glamorous amorous weekend in Paris with him. There was the fulfilment of her ambition to do a scientific job in America And then . . .

Fran knew all about Perdita now. In the taxi she had made Rod tell her. Amazing to think that a girl who looked as though she could have modelled clothes, had been a scientist – an intellectual.

What had she seen in Rod? They couldn't have had much in common, Fran thought, and puzzled over the affair. Then she remembered what it was that had drawn *her* to Rodney in the first place, fourteen years ago. That boyish charm that he could ladle out in such quantities. His sense of humour; his intense vitality, his good looks. There had always been something shining about Rodney . . . just as there must have been about Perdita before she was stricken down. They must have looked wonderful together, Fran thought, as though contemplating two strangers in love rather than her husband and his mistress.

Afterwards, when she remembered this hour, it seemed incredible to Fran that she should accept the position so coolly, so unemotionally. But somehow she felt today that she had something in common with Perdita. They had both loved Rodney.

The difficult moment came when Perdita suddenly moaned, stirred, and opened her eyes.

Fran felt her heart twist at the sight of those aquamarine eyes, clouded now, and with little expression, only a vague surprise. They had said she was not suffering. She was well doped. But the colour of those eyes, oh God, throught Fran, *Miranda's eyes.*

Now Fran felt such a lump in her throat that she couldn't speak, but she reached across the bed and held her hand out to Rodney. He took it.

"Ought we to call a nurse?" he whispered.

"I don't think so. Speak to her."

He let go of Fran's hand and bent over Perdita.

He called her by name several times. She must have heard him because she turned those remarkable eyes in his direction but still she said nothing.

Fran took one of her long fine hands. It was very cold. She pressed it between her own. Anything she had felt in the way of animosity toward this girl who had come between Rodney and herself, had faded. She no longer even remembered the part that Perdita had played in Rodney's life, or her own. This was just a young beautiful creature who, as the

Prayer Book expressed it, was about to be 'cut down like a flower', and it filled her with sorrow.

"Perdita," she said. "My dear, what can we do for you?"

The aquamarine eyes examined Fran. There was some movement in the fingers held by Fran. Now she spoke. So faintly that Fran had to bend close to hear her.

"Hullo," she whispered.

This simple word moved Fran more than anything else could have done. She found it heartbreaking.

"Hullo," she made herself answer in return.

"Who . . . are you?"

"I'm Fran . . . I've come with Rodney to see if we can do anything for you."

There was an instant of silence. Rodney sat like a figure of stone, as though unable to move or speak. Perdita whispered again:

"Rod's . . . wife."

"Yes."

"Why?"

"Why have I come? Just to see if I can do anything for you, Perdita, and to tell you that I don't mind at all about you and Rod."

Perdita seemed to be struggling with her thoughts. Her lashes fluttered. Several times her lips moved but no sound came. But she looked at Fran and not at Rodney, she said:

"Thank you . . . for coming . . ."

Fran pressed the long cold hand.

"What can I do for you? Tell me, *please* tell me."

Perdita seemed to ignore this request.

"I'm dying," she said quite clearly now. "Did you know?"

Rodney leaned forward and touched her hair. Fran glanced at him. She felt nothing but compassion. He really did look awful. Unhappy, wretched Rodney. Perdita spoke to him in a whisper:

"Poor Rod . . . so mixed-up."

He had nothing to say, so Fran spoke for him.

"He loves you very much, Perdita. I know that."

Perdita actually managed a small laugh.

"Funny. You're much . . . much nicer than I am. So . . . kind."

"I'm not," said Fran hastily. "I'm always being horrid to Rod."

Perdita shut her eyes and gave a long sigh.

"Isn't it a waste?" she whispered. "All I've learnt . . . my good brain . . . such a ghastly waste. That's what I resent . . . not my actual death."

Rodney got up.

"Sorry, Fran, I can't take it. I'll wait for you outside."

He bent, touched Perdita's cheek with his lips and moved away.

Fran half rose, meaning to call a nurse, but Perdita said:

"Don't . . . leave me."

Fran sat back in her chair. She took the girl's hand between her own again, bent over her and smoothed back the shining hair which was damp with sweat.

"Dear Perdita, can't I do anything at all for you?"

"Nothing. Don't be . . . too cross . . . with Rod."

They were the last words Perdita said. She did not speak again. When the Sister came at Fran's call, she told her that Perdita was no longer breathing.

So, Fran thought in a daze, beautiful Perdita for whom Rod had almost left her and Peter, had died just like that, holding *her* hand. What an irony!

She began to cry as she walked out of the Ward and started to look for Rodney.

17

HUSBAND and wife did not speak on the return journey from the hospital to their home.

Once back, Rodney went to his own room and shut the door. Fran respected his wish to be alone. Her own tears had dried.

Once more she had become the practical person she usually was, and before leaving the hospital she had discussed with the Almoner what had best be done for Miss Shaw.

She did not ask Rodney what to do. She knew him. He had a horror of death and funerals. He had flinched from going even to his own mother's cremation. He would be only too pleased for Fran to take charge from now onwards. After all, the Perdita he had loved and wanted so madly was no longer alive. He would not want to see her after they had laid her out; of that Fran was sure. It was best, Fran suggested to the Almoner, that they should wait definite news from New Zealand, from Perdita's aunt, before making final arrangements.

"I'll also let them know at this place where Miss Shaw used to work," she told the Almoner. "Once we have heard from her aunt, we'll discuss the funeral."

The Almoner looked at the slim pale woman and admired her dignity.

"It's very good of you to be doing this really, Mrs. Grifford. I understand you haven't known that poor young girl all that long."

Fran had had to take a grip of herself in order not to burst into an hysterical laugh. What, she wondered, would the woman have thought, had she told her that she had never really known Perdita Shaw at all, and had looked upon her for the first time on the day of her death, and that it was her husband who had been the girl's lover.

She asked the Almoner if she could open Perdita's bag and suitcase that the Police had put in the ambulance after the accident, and see if she could find the address of the aunt in New Zealand. The Almoner found it in the dead girl's diary. '*Aunt Liz*', then, in brackets, *Mrs. Cornhill, 22, Hepburn Court, Leelong Avenue, Auckland.*

Afterwards, Fran cabled Mrs. Cornhill.

"*Deeply regret to inform you of Perdita Shaw's death following fatal accident in London this morning. Please cable instructions to her friend, Mrs. Rodney Grifford . . .*"

And to this Fran added her own address.

She might as well make it all look respectable and above-board for the poor aunt, she thought with compassion, and certainly Rodney would not want to be implicated now.

Once home, she telephoned Perdita's office. She knew the number because the Almoner had handed her a business letter from one of the directors, John Coolham who had sent it to Miss Shaw, accepting her notice.

Fran asked to speak to Mr. Coolham. He was not available but his secretary took the message and said that she would see that he received it immediately.

"What a *dreadful* thing! Miss Shaw was so wonderful. So gorgeous to look at, too, and *brilliant* at her work."

Fran closed her eyes.

"Yes."

"I can't *believe* it," the secretary went on. "She was only here this time yesterday – absolutely full of her plans for the future. I can't *believe* that anybody so vital can be dead."

"These car accidents are ghastly," said Fran quietly.

"May I tell Mr. Coolham who has telephoned, please?"

"Yes, say it's a Mrs. Rodney Grifford. You'll find my telephone number in the directory if he wants to ring me."

"I'm sure he will, Mrs Grifford. May I say who you are? A relative of Miss Shaw's — ?"

Fran's mouth twisted into an utterly wretched smile.

"I suppose you could call me that. Anyhow, my husband and I . . ." she stumbled over those words . . . "have just seen Miss Shaw at the hospital . . . she sent for us, and I've cabled her aunt, her next-of-kin, who is in Auckland."

"Yes, we all knew she had relatives in New Zealand, and we knew Mr. Robert Morrison who was with her in the car. How dreadful to think he's dead, too."

"Well, if you don't mind just giving Mr. Coolham the message," ended Fran, feeling utterly exhausted, but the girl at the other end of the wire seemed hungry for more morbid details.

Why had Miss Shaw died? What were her injuries? Of course Mr. Morrison must have been driving. When would the funeral be? On and on, until Fran could endure no more.

With an apology, she said goodbye, hung up, and rather bitterly reflected that it seemed a bit much that she should be doing Rodney's job for him. For it was Rodney who had known and loved Perdita. Rodney who had been closer to her than all her other friends.

But Rodney wouldn't have wanted to take a hand in this tricky situation, and Fran knew it.

Suddenly, she realised that neither she nor Rodney had had any lunch. It was now four o'clock.

Rodney had looked pretty grim when they got back. It would be a good thing to give him some sort of meal. So, in her practical way, she made some coffee and cut some sandwiches; luckily they had a few slices of ham in the fridge.

She took a tray up to Rodney.

He had taken off his coat and was lying on the bed with his face buried in the pillow.

It was strange, thought Fran, but she felt no jealousy now – no resentment at the sight of his grief for another woman. She refused to be jealous of the dead. She had really felt quite maternal when she had smoothed the beautiful golden hair back from that marble forehead. She had in some curious way taken the place of Perdita's mother . . . just as she had been Miranda's.

"Rod," she said gently, "try and get this down. You haven't eaten all day. Do try not to let yourself go too far down."

He turned and looked at her. He, too, had aged in these few hours, she thought. He was white and red-eyed, and had lost all his self-confidence.

"I don't want anything to eat – I want a drink —' he began.

She interrupted:

"Listen . . . I'm not fetching you brandy. No use getting tight. Have some strong black coffee even if you don't eat the sandwiches."

He glared at her.

"Why don't you leave me alone?"

Now she was moved to anger in the face of such ingratitude, but even then tried to rationalise the affair, and tell herself that he was hardly in his right mind just now, and that she oughtn't to take offence at anything he did or said.

She put the tray down beside him.

"I won't disturb you again," she said wearily.

He sat up, tugging at his tie and pulling it off. His lips worked.

"Oh, I'm sorry, Fran. I really don't know what I am saying or doing."

"That is precisely what I thought."

"You can't want to be with me, anyway," he said childishly. "You've been acting like a goddam saint . . . but you aren't one. You're just trying to be awfully kind. And you're human. I know you, and you must loathe my guts."

She gave a deep sigh.

Her eye was caught and held by the sight of the coat that Rod had thrown on the floor. Automatically she stooped, picked it up, and hung it over the back of a chair.

"That's right," he said bitterly. "Do everything you can. Be nice to me. Cover my head with ashes if it makes you feel any better."

She shook her head.

"You're really no older than Pete," she said. "He behaves just like this when he gets upset and pushes me away because I'm trying to comfort him."

"Well, I'm not Pete. I'm your husband and a bloody bad one. Why don't you say something unpleasant – why don't you tell me that you hate my guts?"

"Because, in fact, I don't. I agree I'm no plaster saint. There have been moments when I've wanted to pack up and walk out of this house and never see you again. Nobody likes to go on being hurt. But I thought we'd agreed that as long as our son was at school we wouldn't split up. So what would have been the good of me raving and ranting at you? You meant to go to Paris with *her*. And now she'd dead. Why should I want to be venomous about her now? I knew all about her before she died, didn't I?"

He sat on the edge of the bed pressing his hands down on either side. Hadn't Perdita told him, many times, that he was a poor psychologist and didn't understand women? Too true! He didn't. And least of all did he understand his wife. But as he dragged himself for a second out of the morass of self-pity that followed the shock and horror of Perdita's death, he saw how tired Fran looked – tired and ill. Her eyes were sunk. He felt that the wall of hostility, coldness, and misunderstanding between them was building up and up and that soon he wouldn't see her at all. She would most certainly leave him; even if he didn't leave her.

He turned away and threw himself back on the bed.

"I deserve anything you like to say to me, but I just can't take much more for the moment," he said.

She went out of the room and shut the door. She did not see him again for the rest of that afternoon. Passing his door on one occasion she heard him snoring. She shrugged her shoulders. How nice to be a man and to be able to fall asleep even in the face of dire tragedy.

I wish I could sleep, she thought.

She went to her desk after a cup of tea and started a letter to Pete.

She got as far as:

> "*Daddy and I are very well and busy. Daddy has a special lot to do so don't be surprised if he doesn't write this week. He sends his love with mine. He hopes the maths are going better. Isn't it a pity you didn't inherit his good financial brain instead of my love of classics? . . .*

Then she put down her pen. A feeling of absolute despair suddenly swept over her and carried her a long way from the cheerful practical note she was trying to introduce into her letter.

Daddy and I, oh God, how long could this farce of a marriage go on? Whether the girl who had disturbed Rodney's life so disastrously was alive or dead, her influence was still very much alive. She was here in this house with him. Fran felt it. She was upstairs in his room where he had been sweating out his grief and was now sleeping. Perdita's spirit had come to haunt them both.

And what of *her* grief, her loss?

Fran's face was suddenly drenched in bitter tears. She could not finish the letter to her son. She could not go on writing all those lies, trying to impress Pete that his parents weren't quarrelling any more, and that all was well, and that he need not fear divorce.

What did she really feel about Rodney? Did she still love him? Even though she was sorry for him, how could she feel anything but resentment and even contempt? And why not go away and live alone with Peter somewhere, instead of acting a lie all the time. It was killing her.

She cried until her head throbbed and her nose was stuffed up, and she felt sick and cold.

She decided to do nothing about the evening meal. If Rodney wanted one later on, he would have to go out and get it. He wasn't the only one who could enjoy the luxury of shutting himself away in his bedroom and sleeping. That was what she would do now.

Aching in every limb she undressed, and lay in a very hot bath, then she took a sleeping tablet and went to bed. She felt that if she couldn't forget everything for a while she would crack up and that's one thing she mustn't do. She had to keep going – for Pete.

The hot bath and the sleeping pill had their effect. She went out like a light, and knew nothing until she heard Rodney calling her name.

He was shaking her. His voice sounded sharp and frightened.

"Fran! *Fran!* Wake up."

She looked up at him in a bemused way, blinking.

"Wha' is it? Whas a' matter?"

"Oh, thank God!" he said, confusing her.

Fully awake now, she saw that it was night. The curtains were drawn and the electric bedside-lamp was burning. Rodney seated himself on the bed beside her and looked down at her in silence. He seemed to have recovered, she thought. He was dressed and he had shaved and brushed that thick shining hair that she used to find so attractive.

She sat up.

"What time is it, then?" she asked.

He looked at his wrist-watch.

"Ten o'clock. You've been lying here like a log for hours."

"Heavens!"

"I went to sleep myself, and when I woke up, I looked in on you. Saw you were sleeping, so I didn't disturb you. Then I saw that bottle of sleeping pills, and you were lying so still, I was afraid . . . afraid you . . ." He stammered and broke off, got up and moved away. "Dammit," he said in a hoarse voice. "You gave me a fright."

Now Fran understood. She laughed.

"Don't laugh like that!" He almost snarled the words.

"Well, I can't go on crying," she began, but he broke in.

"You gave me a fright," he said again. "Dammit, I've had enough for one day."

"Don't tell me you were scared you might be going to lose *me* as well," she began with a sarcasm totally foreign to her. Then she was remorseful. "Oh, all right – I'm sorry I scared you. But I did not take an overdose, I assure you."

"I was just afraid you might have done," he said sullenly. "That's all."

"With Peter in the world, I'm not likely to try and take my life," Fran said, swung her legs over the side of the bed, and got up. She felt better after that long sleep but her head ached abominably.

"I should have realised that," said Rodney. "Sorry for making such a fool of myself."

"I'm sorry I gave you a fright," she said politely.

He gave her a long miserable look.

Suddenly she said:

"I'm afraid I'm being rather beastly."

"Yes, you've changed the hell of a lot, Fran. I blame myself, of course. It's all my fault."

She walked to the dressing-table, sat down, and began to brush her dark short hair. He watched her, unhappily.

Unimaginative though Rodney was, he had always possessed a certain warmth of feeling, a rather fatal and pathetic wish to please everybody. If it could have been arranged, he would like to have kept both his wife and his mistress happy. Now he faced the disastrous truth; he had made neither of them happy. He had even loved Perdita more than she had loved him. Hadn't she been on the verge of leaving him, in her cool casual way? Even now that she was dead, it irked him to remember the things she had said only the last time they were together.

"Won't you miss me at all?" he had asked, hungry for the flattery she so rarely gave. She answered:

"Of course, idiot! You know perfectly well I find you a most satisfactory lover. But I've always told you that I'm not the average female slave. I think something must have gone wrong with my genes. There's so much male in me and as dear old Byron said: '*Man's love is of man's life a thing apart.*' Well, so it is in mine so you ought to understand." And she laughed and changed the subject.

She wanted to show him an illustrated textbook that had just come from America with staggering coloured photographs of the new fantastic computer she was going to work on in the New York office. Yes, she had more than a touch of the masculine. Yet she was so devastatingly female when she wanted to be. She had turned the tables upon Rodney. *He* had become the slave.

"It's a good thing I'm going, really. It might give you a chance to make poor Fran a bit happier," she said.

It was a chance he ought to take. Yet what had he done except behave monstrously to his wife in the face of her loyalty and devotion?

Once he had loved Fran above all other women. Even now, despite her sarcasm, and her change of heart toward him, he had an idea that she was still vulnerable where he was concerned. And she had been unbelievably good and generous when Perdita was dying. He felt a strong wish to show his gratitude. He did not know what to do, but he came closer to her.

"Fran," he said, "I would like you to believe that it would have finished everything for me tonight if you'd really tried to kill yourself."

She went on brushing her hair, with swift nervous strokes. At last she looked at his reflection in the mirror, and gave a quick ironic smile.

"Oh, no. I find that a little difficult to swallow, Rod."

"Don't be awkward!" he broke out angrily. "Why should I want you to die?"

"Well, not today perhaps. Obviously you wouldn't want to lose us *both* the same day."

He looked at her now in horror. He would never have believed Fran capable of such venom. He began to stammer:

"If it makes you feel better to say that sort of thing . . . *oh Christ* . . you must hate me. But it can't make you feel good. It's the most awful thing I've ever heard *anyone* say."

He broke off and began to walk out of the room. Fran dropped her brush. She was suddenly filled with horror at herself, and with remorse. She ran after him and caught his arm with both hands.

"Rod, don't go. That was unforgivable of me. I don't know what made me say it. Please forget it. I suppose it's because I've been so unhappy and tensed up."

She felt him relax. He turned back to her and she was even more horrified to see that his eyes were full of tears. She said:

"Rod, I do know what you're going through, honestly. I *am* sorry – truly I am."

"You needn't be. I deserve the lot and I got the lot," he said, pulled away from her and took a handkerchief out of his pocket and blew his nose violently.

She said nothing but hung her head. She felt ashamed. Knowing that that poor beautiful girl was lying there in the mortuary in the hospital, she really must not continue to play the injured wife. How could she have been so ungenerous to her own husband whom she was supposed to have loved so much? And even if the word '*love*' no longer came into it, she should, at least, show some sort of tolerance today.

She said with gentleness:

"Come downstairs, Rod. Open a bottle of wine. We both need it. And I'll cook some eggs and bacon. You haven't really eaten all day. Neither of us has. Come on, Rod, let's have some supper together and don't let's fight tonight. It's exactly what *she* didn't want."

He stared into Fran's big, swimming eyes.

"What *who* didn't want?"

"Perdita."

He went scarlet.

"*Perdita*. What on earth do you mean?"

Fran turned from him.

"Well, it was rather amazing, really – it amazed me. After you'd gone I asked her if there was anything she wanted and she said 'Don't be cross with poor Rod'. It was the last thing she said before she died."

He stood very still, digging his nails into the palms of his hands. In that second he could really see why Perdita had always accused him of not being able to understand women. That Perdita with her dying breath should tell his wife not to be cross with him, seemed quite incomprehensible. And very touching.

Fran took his hand and pulled him through the doorway.

"Come on, come downstairs with me. Whatever happens to us in the future, let's try to be friends tonight."

He did not know whether he loved or hated her for being so nice to him. But he did know that he was in desperate need of her friendliness, and that he could not have borne this black period of his life if she had gone on being unkind, no matter how much he deserved it.

They ate their eggs and bacon and drank their coffee in the kitchen where it was warm and the light was bright. They talked with some embarrassment at first, then more naturally as in the old days when they ate late supper in here like this. Of course, they discussed their son, and Rodney made a particular point of saying how pleased he was that in Pete's last letter he had said that he was taking to rugger these days. He was going to practise hard in order to get into the Colts XV, and he had hoped Daddy would be pleased because Daddy had been rather good at rugger when he was Pete's age.

"That's the best news I've had for a long time," remarked

Rodney. "He used to be such a little wet about games. I think he's toughening up."

Fran, elbows on the table, thin small hands gripping her coffee cup, sipped some of the hot liquid and gave her husband the faintest smile.

"I agree. You can't get through life – especially today– if you aren't a bit tough. But I really never expected it of Pete."

"What's brought about the change do you think?"

"Oh, I think because he's lately had a 'thing' about his father. It was too much *me* at one time but you were so nice to him at Christmas, he was thrilled – you know what boys are – and now he wants to copy you."

Rodney lit a cigarette and stared at the end of it.

"That's the last thing I want him to do."

Now suddenly Fran wanted to defend her husband and did so with sincerity, her large brown eyes warm as she looked at him.

"Oh, for God's sake don't Rod. There are heaps of things about you I'd like Peter to copy."

Rodney gave a dry laugh.

"I won't ask you to name them. I know you think I'm too damned full of myself – you've said so plenty of times, but I promise you I'd rather he took after *you*."

She set her empty cup down in the saucer, got up and made a clatter of stacking dirty plates. She could not possibly let Rodney see how his praise warmed her starved heart. She felt that it was tragic she had had to wait for a night like this in order to receive it. To cover her embarrassment, she spoke rather sharply.

"Oh well, we can't sit here saying nice things to each other. You go on into the sitting-room and smoke your cigar in peace and I'll put these few things in the machine."

He pushed back his chair and stood up. The sentimental moment had passed. He felt as she did, the sudden chill in the air. The chill that blows from the mountaintop of truth. And the truth was that he had betrayed Fran who was trying in her own especial gallant way to cover up for him, and that although he loved her in his sorry fashion, he had loved Perdita more. It was a perfectly terrifying thought that now, suddenly, all that beauty and wit and intelligence – all the loveliness that he had held so often in his arms – were no more. She had been wiped off the earth. He would never see her or speak to her again.

For the first time since he was a young boy at his Confirmation, he wished desperately that he still believed in Life after Death.

As he walked out of the kitchen he heard Fran's voice:

"Rod, I've been meaning to tell you for ages, one of the screws in the roller-towel holder has come out. Do you think you can find another screw and bung it in for me?"

He put the back of his hand against his forehead as though trying to clear his brain. That simple request seemed so silly, yet it was steadying after the events of the day.

He found the screw, put in a fresh rawlplug, and completed the job.

"Thanks," said Fran who was drying spoons and forks.

He looked at the straight back. A gallant back. Really if Fran wasn't his wife he would want to hug her. What other woman did he know who would be behaving like this? Who would have been as kind and charitable as she at the deathbed of her husband's mistress?

He walked out of the kitchen and up to his own room rather than to the sitting-room. He really felt he must be alone again. He couldn't bear another hour of artificial mundane conversation with Fran, and anyhow it was quarter to eleven. Even if he couldn't sleep, he must lie down. His whole body seemed to have been jarred, like his mind, and the more he thought about Perdita, the more he began to realise the enormity of his loss. It was as though he had been stunned but now was conscious again. It wasn't a pleasant awakening.

I had what was coming to me, he thought. *You can't play a dirty trick on a woman like Fran and not pay for it. The bloody thing is that I'm the one who should have been killed, not Perdita.*

He took off his coat and hung it over a chair as Fran had done earlier today, shutting his eyes. He wondered what old George would say when he heard that Perdita had been killed. He wouldn't care, of course, as he hardly knew her, although he would be as shocked as anyone by the untimely death of a young and beautiful creature.

He wondered how he was going to go to the Stock Exchange tomorrow and behave as though nothing out of the ordinary had happened. Still more gloomily did he look to the future – to the continuance of this game of '*Let's Pretend*' with his wife, until such time as she chose to divorce him.

If it hadn't been for Peter and his mother's passionate belief that broken homes did so much to hurt the young – leave a mark that came out in some harmful way in the years to come – Rodney would have left home tomorrow. It was almost unbearable to have to stay here in this house with Fran's pervading spirit of forgiveness. To go on exchanging visits and parties with their friends, and behave as though he were a happily married man.

He turned and saw the two photographs that Fran had left on his chest of drawers. He picked up Perdita's and a physical pain tore at his very guts.

"God!" he said aloud. "*God!*" And it was with a queer sensation of astonishment that he endured such pain. He had not thought himself capable of loving any woman in this way. And then he argued with himself that his great passion for her could never have come to anything anyhow because she had wanted to live with him but not to marry him. And she had not really loved him.

He dropped Perdita's photograph as though it burned his fingers. He picked up Miranda's. His eyes were bloodshot as he stared down at that small adorable face. He hadn't permitted himself to look at it since the day of her death.

Gradually it seeped into his mind that he must have been brutally unconscious in the past of the full extent to which Fran must have suffered, believing that she was, in a way, responsible for the little girl's death. Again and again she had wept in his arms, blaming herself for the accident.

He let Miranda's photograph fall upon Perdita's.

"I've lost them both," he said. "There must be something terrible about me and I'm being punished for it."

He was not an impulsive man but suddenly he acted on impulse. He had the strongest desire to exonerate Fran from all blame. Even if his pain went on for the rest of his life, why must hers?

He went downstairs and called to her.

"Fran, I want to speak to you."

She came out of the kitchen, a cigarette between her lips. She looked very tired and pale. She took the cigarette in her fingers.

"What can I do for you?"

"Fran —" he began, and stopped.

She looked at him, head a little on one side, questioningly.

"What is it, Rod?"

His face coloured. He stammered:

"Fran, I want to tell you . . ."

"Yes, what?"

"I don't know," he muttered, "*I don't know.*"

She sighed deeply. She could so easily have felt no pity. He had brought this grief upon himself and spoiled her life. But in this moment she was truly sorry for him, thinking, mistakenly, he was trying to say something about the girl.

"Don't think about it any more tonight, Rod. Poor Perdita seems to have had a brilliant life. It might all have been a disappointment if she'd lived. In a way, I think it must be nice to die at the height of success and before you can suffer badly as some people do when they grow old."

"I wasn't going to say anything about Perdita."

"Then what?"

He stared down into the soft brown eyes which he had once found so entrancing. Lately they had annoyed him because their very softness made him feel guilty.

Then he said in a stumbling way:

"It was actually about Miranda. I want you to know. I want you to know —"

"Don't," she broke in, and her face seemed to freeze. "Don't say any more – not tonight."

"But I've got to," he said violently. "It's all come over me that I've *got to.* I don't think I've ever really said this, but I want to say it now – to ask you to believe it's the truth – that I've never held Miranda's death against *you* – never! Or if I did for a split second, it was because I was so shattered. But I know you only left her for a few seconds. Anybody might have done that. *I* would have. Don't ever think that I really held it against you or that it was because of *her* that I fell in love with somebody else."

Fran was speechless for a moment. She looked as though he had struck her rather than tried to comfort her. Her face screwed up.

"But you did fall in love with Perdita because she reminded you of Miranda, didn't you?"

"Maybe," he said in a hoarse voice. "Maybe. I don't know. I don't know anything any more."

Another silence. Fran put a clenched fist against her mouth. Despite all her control the tears began to pour down her cheeks.

"Anyhow what does it matter now? Whatever you felt about Perdita – or Miranda, if it comes to that – you fell out of love with me."

He gave her a helpless look, wondering what to say, because he didn't want to be dishonest any longer – he wanted there to be absolute truth between them.

Then Fran said in a strangled voice:

"Thanks for trying to be nice to me."

Before he could speak again, she pushed past him and ran up the stairs. He heard her bedroom door close.

They did not see or speak to each other again that terrible night.

18

DURING the week that followed, the Locks asked them to a dinner and Bridge party which Fran refused because Rodney said he couldn't face it, even if she could. This, of course, brought a barrage of questions from Harriet.

"Why on earth not? You've forgotten I asked you to keep that date until I let you know whether I could get hold of John and Betty Dickens. Honestly, Fran, it'll be a great disappointment to me as I've fixed the Dickens now and they wanted to meet you. It's almost impossible to get a busy Q.C. like John without a lot of notice."

When Fran trumped up a story about an old friend of Rod's having died, and he was upset and didn't want to go out, Harriet, who knew them both well enough, persisted in questioning.

"Well, is it the day of the funeral? Can't Rod make an effort?"

Then when Fran still refused, Harriet became curious.

"What's up with you two? Come clean, Fran darling. We've been friends for years. Something's wrong?"

Fran stoutly denied this and after a few difficult seconds managed to shake Harriet off. She was very fond of Harriet, but how could she begin to tell her the truth? After all, it wasn't so much her story as Rod's, and if they were going to make a happy home for Peter for the next year or two it wouldn't do to circulate the smallest suggestion that their marriage was on the rocks.

She tried to feel grateful because he had absolved her from blame of Miranda's death . . . suddenly, after eight long years. But she wondered whether it was because he had been a bit off-balance that he had tried to be especially nice to her.

At the beginning of that week a cable came from Perdita's aunt, announcing that she was flying over to England with her husband. She also asked that Perdita's kind friends would arrange the cremation.

Fran saw her husband's face when he read this cable. She said hastily:

"You needn't even meet them. I'll say you're ill and I'll deal with Aunt Liz. After all, it *must* be me and not you, mustn't it?"

"You're the most astonishing person, Fran. Why? —"

"Listen," she broke in. "You know I'm not a malicious person and I don't honestly feel anything but sorrow about that girl. I don't want you implicated and I can quite easily act a part to satisfy her aunt."

He made the gesture of a man who failed to understand but was deeply grateful.

"For God's sake, don't come to the cremation, either,' added Fran.

"Oughtn't I to?"

"Do you want to?"

He turned from her. He felt sick.

"You know I bloody don't. I'm not as courageous as you."

She pitied him. Always she seemed to be sorry for Rod. *After all*, she thought, *if I'd had a lover and he'd been killed and I'd been made to act a part in front of his family*, *I don't think I could have done it.*

"Don't worry, Rod – I'll represent the Griffords. You can be ill," she said.

When Mrs. Cornhill arrived in London with her husband Rod's 'illness' had already started, and the Cornhills accepted without questioning, that he was 'laid up with flu'. In any case they took it for granted that Frances Grifford had been Perdita's friend.

On the day they landed, Fran met them in Brown's Hotel where she had booked a room for the Cornhills.

Mrs. Cornhill proved to be in her late forties, thin, rather wrinkled, and very tall. Height ran in the family, she told Fran. Poor darling Perdita had, of course, been of exceptional height.

Fran was thankful that she had little to do but sit and listen to 'Aunt Liz' who never stopped talking. At least there was nothing about her to remind Fran of Perdita. She was a nice but rather boring woman. But she had strong family feeling and seemed to have adored her niece who had lived with her when she was a little girl.

After Perdita's mother died, Mrs Cornhill's brother, Professor Shaw, spent most of his time travelling and lecturing abroad, she told Fran. Perdita had inherited his intellect.

"She was mad about science and mathematics when she was at school. Such an odd child."

"Yes," said Fran stonily.

Mr. Cornhill had gone out shopping. He seemed as dull as his wife, but nice. He greatly embarrassed Fran by kissing her on both cheeks when they first met, and thanking her for being 'so good to his wife's poor niece'.

The whole thing had a queer effect upon her. The image in which she had cast herself as Perdita's friend, in order to spare the aunt's feelings as well as Rodney's reputation, had become reality. She was beginning to feel that she had really known the girl quite well. With unashamed curiosity she looked at some of the photographs Mrs. Cornhill had brought over to show her. She was especially moved by one of Perdita as a child. *There*, certainly, the resemblance to Miranda was strong, and twisted the old knife in Fran's heart. She wished she could show some of the other ones to Rodney. He must have adored her golden beauty. In her teens, Perdita's body looked so splendid; 'Dita' as her aunt called her, in her bikini suit surf-bathing, or diving from the rocks. 'Dita' playing tennis. 'Dita' in cap and gown fresh from Oxford, looking grave and oh, so intelligent!

"To think," said Aunt Liz, wiping her eyes, "that it's all ended, and she had so much to give."

"That's what she said," Fran told her.

"Did she mention me?" asked Aunt Liz wistfully.

"Yes, and she sent you her love."

"Darling Dita. What did she say at the end?"

Fran turned away. Dear God, she thought, she could hardly repeat Perdita's last words:

'*Don't be cross with Rod.*'

Feeling under considerable strain – she made up a few words. But she got away from the hotel and Aunt Liz as soon as she could.

She felt quite upset. She was glad that she had several hours in which to recover before Rodney got back from the Stock Exchange. She told him that she liked Mrs. Cornhill very much; that it was obvious Perdita had never mentioned *him*, and that everything was all right.

"I can't tell you how much I admire you for doing this —" he began.

"You look tired," broke in Fran. "I'll get you a whisky."

She felt quite unable to bear any emotional talks with Rod.

She dreaded the funeral, but got through it, exerting all her powers of self-control. She was thankful that Rodney had actually had to leave town suddenly and go up to the Lake District to see a wealthy old gentleman to whom he was financial adviser, and who was ill and had sent for him. That suited Fran. She felt that she could do with an evening quite alone – especially after this morbid day.

The Cornhills asked her to dinner, but she refused.

Once at home, alone, she felt less tense, but could not shut out the cynical thought that today, at least, she need not feel torn with jealousy or anger because she was afraid Rodney had gone away with his girl-friend. The trip to Windermere was genuine business this time.

She hoped the Cornhills would go home soon. She really could not bear much more of Aunt Liz's rapturous memories of Perdita.

The worst was yet to come.

The Cornhills made arrangements to fly back to Auckland at the end of the following week. If Aunt Liz asked Fran to another meal, Fran had meant to refuse, but there came a morning when Aunt Liz, her voice sounding a trifle odd, was insistent.

"Please come if you can, Frances. I – I'm rather upset. I must see you."

Fran, none too happy, thought: *Now what's happened?*

But she could not refuse Aunt Liz's request.

It was a cold bright February day with a strong wind. Fran put on a fur coat, tied a scarf over her hair, and took a taxi to the hotel.

The moment she saw Aunt Liz – who had begged her to call her by that name – she could sense a change in her. She had always been rather soft and sentimental and weepy about Perdita and on several occasions gripped Fran's hand or made some other little gesture of warmth. Today she greeted Fran in a strained fashion.

"Come and sit down," she said, adding, "My husband is at

the tailor's. They don't make suits in Auckland the way they do in London, you know."

"I'm sure they don't," said Fran, and sat down, loosened her coat, unwound the scarf, pushing back a wind-blown lock of hair.

Mrs. Cornhill look dubiously at the younger woman.

"Oh dear, I haven't slept all night," she said. "I've found it very difficult indeed to decide whether or not to tell you about this. Then I talked it over with my husband who is extraordinarily perceptive, and do you know what he said?"

Fran shook her head. She didn't for the moment know what Mrs. Cornhill was talking about.

"He said that he was perfectly sure that you already *knew*, and that you were being very brave, trying to cover up for your husband and spare me. I'm sure you *must* know – Dita suggested in her diary that you did."

Fran's heart sank. She rolled her eyes heavenwards. Oh God, why did people keep diaries? It ought to have gone out of date with all the other mistakes the Victorians made. But it hadn't. People still jotted down their secret thoughts and actions and there could be no greater form of egotism – or, in its way, was it not the purest luxury of confession, even of confessing to oneself? Always irrespective of the fact that it might one day be read and misconstrued or hurt the unsuspecting person.

Aunt Liz went on talking.

She had decided, she said, that she could not go back to New Zealand without talking this over with Fran. Not because she wanted to make trouble between Frances and her husband but because she hoped to remedy it. She intended to ensure that what her niece had done would not break up their marriage.

"It's all been a great shock to me," she ended, and gratefully accepted a cigarette from the packet that Fran offered. She did not drink but she liked smoking.

Fran, too, lit a cigarette and for a few seconds the two women smoked in silence. Then Fran went into action. She had never been one to shirk an unpleasant duty when it was necessary.

"Don't let's avoid truths. Let's lay the cards on the table,

Aunt Liz," she said. "You obviously know about your niece and my husband."

"Yes, I do. It's all in here —" She pulled a polished pigskin, gilt-edged diary from her bag. "I've read a few pages. *Enough*," she added. "Rather stupidly thinking it would be just a record of Dita's work, but after a few pages I saw Rodney's name. Dita described her meeting with him at some supper-party given by a man . . . what was his name . . . oh, yes – Stirling."

"Yes," nodded Fran, "George Stirling – a friend on the Stock Exchange with my husband."

She felt chilled despite the warmth of the lounge, and reluctant to open the dead girl's diary that Aunt Liz handed her. But she would have been less than human if she hadn't flipped through one or two pages. She soon recognised the cool scientific approach, even to a love-affair. Unsentimental – and unflattering to Rod – just plain and sometimes rather brutal truths.

"*In some ways I find him attractive, but abominably conceited. I was amused at his efforts to dig some response out of me . . .*"

Thought Fran: *That must have shaken Rod . . . he was so sure, always, that he could make the grade with the girls. Poor Rod!*

She could see that he hadn't made the grade with Perdita at all to start with, and it was even painful to Fran to read some of Dita's witty, barbed allusions to his overtures. Finally her attention was caught and held by one small page (and God how *that* hurt), a fantastically unsentimental memorandum of the first time they had become lovers.

"*He's rather better in bed than my don. Rod is really out of this world but he's a bit of a bore with all his oh Gods, and telling me I'm so marvellous, etc. I told him the young don't go on like that. But he's more vital than my former boy-friend —*"

Pale and trembling, Fran snapped the diary together and handed it back to Mrs. Cornhill.

"I don't want to see any more. Please take it. Burn it. It ought to be burnt."

"I agree. I've only read enough to show me that Dita was living with him in her flat at times. I really was only interested in the dates before she died. The last recording said that she had decided to break away from him after their visit to Paris."

Fran nodded and wondered whether she would have to make an excuse to go to the Powder Room and be sick. It was almost unbearable, this sudden hateful picture of Perdita behaving like a scientific machine in Rodney's arms. Yet how fascinating she must have been – something so new, so devastating. She hated Perdita today as she had not done when she first learned about the affair.

Mrs. Cornhill leaned forward and touched Fran's knee.

"Did you find something very upsetting? I'm beginning to feel I should never have let you read it. But I wanted you to believe, after reading it, that it's obvious Perdita had no intention of taking your husband away from you. She didn't want to get married to anyone, I'm afraid. If you'd read the end part you'd see she was already growing tired of the affair."

"A bit too late," said Fran harshly. "She'd already taken him from me, hadn't she?"

"No, no, please try to forget that, and forgive him. He wasn't even the first with her. I can see now that she was not like other girls – she had absolutely no moral sense. She wasn't out for a real lasting love-affair. I don't think, my dear, you need ever feel they were lovers in the true sense. I shall forgive Dita because I think death wipes out everything. But please, please, Frances, don't let her break up your home *now*."

Did death wipe out everything? Fran wondered with bitterness, and her fingers shook so badly with cold and nerves that she could hardly hold her cigarette.

"Do you mind if I have some strong black coffee?" she asked.

"Of course, of course, I'll order it, my dear."

Fran sat still, feeling that she hadn't anything left to say. Mrs. Cornhill went on apologising for having let her see the diary, and repeating that her only object in doing so, had been to help Frances realise that it was no ordinary affair, and certainly not one worth breaking up her marriage for.

"You have a son. He wouldn't want his parents to separate, I'm sure," Mrs. Cornhill ended.

"No. He wouldn't. I would have left Rodney some time ago if it hadn't been for our son. He's an awfully nice boy and he has a horror of us divorcing. Some of his friends have had to face up to broken homes and separated parents and it worried Peter. He's rather a sensitive person. My husband and I reached an agreement that we wouldn't, whatever happened, separate until Peter left school."

"Oh, my dear, don't break it up even then —" began Aunt Liz with tears in her eyes. "I feel so terribly dreadfully upset that this has happened because of my niece."

Fran suddenly disliked this stupid woman. She gave a short laugh and sipped her coffee.

"I don't think you need feel responsible for your niece."

"You're such a brave person – such a good one," droned Aunt Liz. "You were truly wonderful the way you stepped into the breach and tried to shield your husband *and* our niece."

"I'm sorry you ever found the diary."

"Yes, I am, too. But I still feel it will have been worth the misery if it can make you realise that what your husband felt for Perdita was obviously only a mad infatuation. It would never have come to anything with Dita. She made that quite plain."

"Yes, she made it plain," said Fran in a small hard voice.

It was odd, she thought, but to her the whole thing had worsened because Perdita hadn't loved Rod, but had just wanted to go to bed with him. People behaved like that all over the place, and thought nothing of it. Yet that Rod should have hurt her, his wife, so cruelly because of a girl who gave him her body, and no heart to go with it, seemed to aggravate the position. She, Fran, had loved him body, heart and soul – an absolute love that he had pushed on one side.

Could she ever forgive him?

Suddenly Fran put her cup down in her saucer, stood up and pulled the chiffon scarf out of her pocket.

"Will you excuse me if I go home? Actually I don't feel awfully well."

Mrs. Cornhill got up and seized Fran by the hands.

"My dear, I feel terribly guilty. I've done the wrong thing. I've made things worse instead of better. Oh, how awful of me!"

Fran looked at the woman's silly anxious face and tried to smile.

"Don't let it worry you. Perhaps it's just as well I do know a few more facts, but although I can't explain it, somehow I could have forgiven Rodney more easily if it hadn't all been on such a low level. The idea that my husband has been so humiliated sort of makes my own humiliation worse."

"Oh dear," repeated Mrs. Cornhill and began to cry.

19

FRAN did not wait to console Perdita's aunt. She ran from the hotel into the cold bright day. She walked down Dover Street and found a cruising taxi at the top of Hay Hill. Once home, she was actually sick – a thing that hadn't happened to her as far back as she could remember. Afterwards she lay on her bed with closed eyes, and tried to reorientate her thoughts and emotions. She reproached herself, speaking the words aloud:

"Pull yourself together, Fran, my girl. At least that diary ought to have shown you that you're much too sentimental and soft to get on in this world. You want to be a hell of a lot harder."

She sobbed into her pillows furiously, with a violent grief that shook her from head to foot. Try as she would, she could not shut out the memory of some of the words Perdita had written, loathing them . . . loathing the scorn which Perdita had felt for Rodney even while she accepted his love. Rodney as the once proud self-confident man, frozen by the girl's own coldness, had changed to a man who had to crawl to her, to beg for more. It nauseated Fran.

She could not bear the idea of her husband coming home tonight as usual, expecting his meal, talking about nothing; both of them carefully avoiding all reference to things as they really were. As far as she could see, from now onwards, she would have to live with the memory of that heartless girl and her diary, and live with a man whom she no longer respected. What sort of a father would Rodney make for Peter in the future? How could she be sure that Perdita's death would put an end to his search for whatever it was he needed from a woman and didn't get from *her*, his wife? When would he betray her and his son again?

In a kind of agony, Fran wrestled with herself, visualising this torture going on and on until she cracked. The misery of whether he would ever come into her room, her bed, again and lie beside her. If she wanted him to now.

What lay ahead of her? She was still young, and she knew from the way other men looked at her, spoke to her, that she was still attractive.

Hadn't George Stirling (George who was responsible for introducing Perdita to Rod), actually told her so when he was dancing with her on New Year's Eve. A whole party of them had gone to the Savoy. A long-standing engagement that she had insisted on Rodney keeping, as he had cancelled so many others. George, a little full of champagne and exuberant spirits, had admired her dress as they danced and put his cheek against hers.

"My favourite girl! I'm always telling Rod how lucky he is."

She had made a suitable comment, then laughed, and said:

"I doubt if Rod thinks himself all that lucky. Men do get a bit bored with their wives sometimes, don't you think, George?"

He had denied this stoutly. Now she wondered even if at that stage George knew about Perdita – knew that for the last nine months Rod had been living with her? Men told each other these things.

So she, herself, had drunk a little more champagne and

danced every dance, including one with a delightful, grey-haired Army Officer one of their friends had brought along. He was on leave from Aden. He was a beautiful dancer and told Fran that he had seldom had a more perfect partner. 'A little piece of thistledown,' he called her.

She had been flattered but laughed.

"There's nothing thistledown about *me.*"

"That was a *façon de parler*," he said, "behind those big brown eyes I see an indomitable spirit."

"A lot you know about me," she jeered.

"It's only what I think," he said. "I've been longing to dance with you the whole evening. You're quite the most attractive woman in our party."

She had been pleased. She would tell Rod. It did something to her ego to be praised even by an entire stranger, and he had capped it by telling her about the Army wives in Aden and what a courageous lot they were.

"Women are wonderful," he ended smiling as the dance finished and he took her back to the table.

Later when he was dancing she had asked their hostess about his background and been told that he was rather a tragic figure. He used to have a wife he adored – a lovely girl younger than himself – and she had died of cancer a year ago.

Curiously enough in this hour of misery, Fran remembered the Army Colonel and his story.

How much more (or less) brutal must it be to watch the human being you most love, die of cancer, than see them growing away from you in life, as she had done with Rodney? It was another sort of death; only the Colonel had his memories, and hers were spoilt.

I must get away from Rod. I can't stay here, she thought.

Suddenly she went to the telephone and rang up the Cadogan Travel Company where Rod usually got their tickets.

At this time it ought to be fairly easy to get a flight to Jersey. She would go over to Aunt Chrissie and perhaps she'd stay there. She'd have to ask Peter to forgive her if she didn't go down for the rest of his exeats. His father would have to take him out. But she'd suffered too much . . . more than enough . . . she couldn't take any more.

Just before she got to the telephone, the bell rang. Trying to control her nervous trembling, she lifted the receiver.

"Yes, who is it?"

Came the sound of pips and coins from a call-box, then:

"It's me, Mum."

Fran drew breath. Her eyes widened with astonishment.

"*Pete! Where are you? Is anything the matter?*"

A hesitant voice answered:

"No – yes – well, *yes.*"

"Where are you?"

"Waterloo Station."

"Waterloo?" Fran repeated, mystified and suddenly concerned. "But why? Why aren't you at school?"

"Well, as a matter of fact I – I buzzed up here on my own."

"Do you mean you've run away?"

"Yes."

"But why? —"

Peter interrupted.

"I say, Mum, I can't explain now because I haven't got any more change for the phone."

"Okay. Take a taxi straight home. Do you hear, Pete? Get a taxi tell him to drive you home and that your mother will pay this end."

Once more Fran had become her practical sensible self. All thoughts of flying to Jersey faded. Pete had run away from school and was on his way home. That was enough to be going on with, and enough to strike a note of dread in her heart, albeit she was delighted at the thought of seeing her son so soon. Hastily Fran creamed her face, put on fresh make-up, brushed her hair, and with the certainty in her mind that Pete would be hungry whatever had happened, went down to the kitchen and rummaged through her stores.

She always kept a few tins ready for an emergency. She found a small tin of tongue and opened it. Pete had a good appetite and he would eat all of this. There was a lettuce in the fridge so she could make a salad, and although he was not keen on cheese there was plenty of fruit *and* a half-finished carton of cream. He liked bananas and cream

Before the taxi arrived from Waterloo with the runaway. Fran had laid the kitchen table and was quite ready for her erring son.

Once he arrived, she paid the taxi and followed her son into the house trying to talk as though nothing was wrong. If there was a crisis – Peter was sure to be in a state of jitters. He wouldn't have run away for nothing. He had never done such a thing in all the years he had been at school.

"What a lovely surprise," she said cheerfully. "Take your coat off and I expect you'd like a coke and a piece of cake. I made a fruit-cake yesterday actually. You know Daddy rather 'digs' cake in the weekend."

Peter said nothing. He took off his coat and school-cap. In the kitchen, he sipped his drink but rejected the cake which further alarmed his mother. Something must be very wrong. Peter adored fruit-cake. Examining him anxiously she saw that he had absolutely no colour and there were dark smudges under his eyes. He looked as though he hadn't slept for nights, and he kept shifting from one foot to the other and rubbing his ankle with his foot. A sure sign with Peter that he was nervous. She knew everything about him, she thought, every little thing, and her heart yearned, but she kept on talking brightly.

"Well, you might as well sit down and tell me why you've come. To what, dear, do we owe this unexpected pleasure?" She laughed artificially. But her efforts to make him relax failed.

He twisted his glass between grubby fingers.

"Where's Dad?"

She stared.

"Dad? At the office of course."

"When will he be home?"

"This evening – as usual."

"Can't I see him before?"

Now Fran was utterly bewildered. She looked into the boy's

dark, large eyes – eyes so like her own – and her heart sank as she saw the misery in them. *Oh God*, she thought, *what has happened to my son?*

Peter sniffed.

"I think I've got a cold coming. I forgot my handkerchief."

"Run upstairs and get one out of Daddy's drawer."

While he was gone, she lit a cigarette and tried to understand why Peter had asked so urgently for his father. She had never known him to do such a thing before. When things went wrong he came to her.

Peter appeared again, blowing his nose and looking even more dejected.

"I suppose I'll get into the hell of a row for doing this," he muttered.

"Sit down," she said.

He sat . . . shuffling with his feet, hands dug in his pockets. Fran noticed now that his grey flannel coat was creased and there was a stain on one lapel. His shirt didn't look very clean either. Really, she thought, these matrons today! At a good Public School where they were paying the earth, couldn't they do better than this? Then she wondered why she was worrying about such trifles.

"Does anybody know you've run away, Peter?"

"No. I just walked out during break, and dashed along to the station, and got a ticket for Waterloo. I haven't spent all my pocket money this term so I had enough."

"Are you in trouble? Can't you tell me about it?" she asked him gently.

Now she saw his face go scarlet. He frowned and lowered his lids.

"Well, as a matter of fact I can't, Mum."

"Why not?" she asked, "Surely you and I are friends, darling. We always have been."

"Oh yes, we are. But I don't want to tell you about *this*."

Now all kinds of awful thoughts darted through Fran's brain. She put a hand up to her cheek and pressed it hard against her teeth. She was filled with dread and curiosity but decided not to ask any more questions for the moment. Peter looked positively scared; afraid, it would seem, of being cross-questioned by her.

"Well, the first thing I had better do is to ring Mr. Inholm," she said, "and tell him where you are."

The name of his Housemaster seemed to upset Peter. He sprang up and almost shouted:

"No, *Mum*, *please* don't do that, whatever you do. He'll be in the hell of a bait with me."

"But, Pete, your absence will have been noticed by now and they'll get the police on to you if you're not found."

Before Peter could speak again, once more the telephone bell rang.

As Fran went out of the kitchen, she looked over her shoulder at her son and said:

"I wouldn't mind betting that's the school, They're sure to contact us."

"Don't tell them where I am."

"Darling, I'm sorry," said Fran, "but I've got to. But I will tell one lie and say you've got a temperature and that I'm keeping you for the night, anyhow."

"Okay," said Peter in a dismal voice.

Mr. Inholm it was. Whatever lay at the back of Fran's mind she was perfectly sure that the nice Housemaster knew nothing whatsoever about Peter's troubles and this was not the time to discuss them, perhaps. Peter was and always had been a highly-strung boy and he would be in a frenzy if he thought his mother was talking about him to Mr. Inholm of all people. So Fran made her announcement brief.

"Yes, he's here – just arrived, Mr. Inholm, safe and sound. I'm deeply sorry if he's caused you alarm . . . yes, he's quite all right except that he has a feverish cold. Just breaking out. I'm going to put him to bed at once, but if his temperature is normal I'll bring him back tomorrow and, of course, I'll get his father to contact you by 'phone this evening . . . No, I haven't found out yet why he ran away. He seems in a highly nervous state. Have you a clue?"

Mr. Inholm said that he hadn't the slightest clue as to why young Grifford had done this. As far as he knew all was well with him although perhaps he had seemed *slightly* less cheerful than usual, and unable to concentrate over his work in *quite* the usual way. Normally he was such a bright lad, etc., etc.

The upshot of the conversation was that Mr. Inholm said he would let the Head know that Grifford was safe, which was all that mattered, and they were sure everything would be all right now and that whatever the trouble was, it could be ironed out.

When Fran returned to the kitchen, she found Peter gnawint at his nails. She seized his right hand, looked at it and tried to joke.

"You must be hungry. All your nails chewed up and your finger-tips look puffy and hideous, you silly chump."

He put the offending hand behind his back and glowered at her. He was altogether so unlike her usually affectionate friendly son, she felt devastated.

"Oh, Peter," she said. "Can't you tell me what's wrong? Why *have* you run away?"

"Please, Mum, don't ask me."

"But, Pete, we *must* know – Mr. Inholm says everything will be all right so long as you just explain."

"I don't want to go back to school."

"Pete, you love your new school. You've said so heaps of times. You know how you always wanted to go to Public School and you seemed to be getting on so well. Daddy was so pleased, too, the other day when he heard about the rugger."

"Well, I don't like it as much as I did," said Peter sullenly, then added: "Can't you 'phone Dad and ask him to come home?"

"You mean you can tell Daddy what the matter is but you won't tell me?"

"Yes."

With deep foreboding, Fran gave up asking further questions.

"Sit down and I'll get your lunch," she said.

"I don't want any."

"Well, you're going to eat it and stop this nonsense," said Fran, growing suddenly tough with her son. She really couldn't imagine what had happened to produce such a metamorphosis in him. But she put a plate of tongue in front of the boy and after both threatening and cajoling, managed to make him eat some of it.

She then sent him to his own room.

"Switch on the radiator. It's cold, and have a look at your stamp collection while I wash-up, then we'll speak to Daddy on the 'phone and ask if he could possibly get back early."

Peter retired to his room.

Fran called her husband's office. He was engaged with a client but when she finally spoke to him and told him what had happened, Rodney seemed quite concerned.

"It isn't like Peter to run off like that. What's wrong, do you think?"

"He won't tell me. He says he only wants to tell *you*."

"Well, well!" came from Rodney. "It must be the first time in his life he prefers to talk to me rather than to you."

"You should be pleased," said Fran coldly.

"Well, I don't know that I'm exactly *pleased*, but if the boy needs me, I'll come, and it must be important, or I'm sure he wouldn't have run away."

"When can I tell him you'll be here?"

"Well, it isn't at all convenient, but I'll see what I can do. Say in an hour's time."

Fran put down the receiver. Rodney was certainly making a concession by leaving his office early. She never remembered him doing such a thing before, to please *her*, anyhow. For the first time she realised that he could not be quite so indifferent to his son as he had appeared in the past. She would have been delighted if she hadn't reached the pitch of almost hating Rodney for the way he had behaved – for the way he had gripped her love by the throat and strangled it.

It was with a sudden sense of shock that she remembered that just before Peter 'phoned from Waterloo, she, too, had been about to run away. From Rodney, from the future.

Well, she couldn't go until tomorrow now – that was certain. Not until she was sure Peter was all right.

The next two hours seemed very long, and she was very

tired, but she tried to behave as she always did with Peter – interesting herself in the things she knew he liked, talking about everything except school. Above all she wanted to quieten him down. They played a game of Backgammon which Peter liked. Then another game. Then Fran went out and bought some comics in Sloane Square. Afterwards she made a cup of tea while the boy read his papers.

She was on edge until she actually heard Rodney's key in the latch of the front door. She ran out to meet him.

He looked down at her.

"Well, what's all this about?" he asked.

"It's for you to find out, and be gentle with him, Rod," she said. "He's in rather a state."

Rodney hung up his coat and hat. He looked pinched and cold, she thought. (She tried not to remember Perdita.)

"What did you think I'd do – take a cane to the boy?" he asked irritably.

"No, I just mean – he's in an odd sort of state. As soon as he got home he said he wanted you."

"As I said over the 'phone, that's something new," said Rodney with a short laugh.

"I suppose a boy does need his father at times."

"Exactly," said Rodney. "And I have a pretty shrewd idea what he's going to tell me."

Fran put two fingers against her lips and her lashes flickered nervously.

"Rod – you don't think – oh, *lord*! . . ."

"Leave it to me," he broke in. "Where is he?"

"Have a cup of tea first, you look frozen."

"I'll have it afterwards. Where's Peter?"

"Up on his bed. I don't think he's very well. He's getting a cold."

Rodney went up the stairs. Fran heard him say:

"Pete! Hello there!"

And after that silence.

Fran went into the kitchen. It seemed to her that whenever she took refuge, it was in her kitchen, among her pots and pans and dishes, performing the domestic duties that were the simple daily chores. And now she began to think about to-night's dinner. She had been in such a state after seeing Mrs. Cornhill this morning, and skipping through Perdita's diary, she hadn't given the evening meal a thought, and finally she had anticipated going away before Rodney came home.

Peter's arrival had changed things. In a moment she'd have to run down to the King's Road and get some chops or steaks for everybody, and a tin of pineapple-chunks – Peter's favourites.

She lit one cigarette, smoked it while she pottered around the kitchen, then lit another. She kept looking up at the ceiling, listening. Not a sound. Those two must still be talking. Frankly she was surprised by the way Rodney was suddenly showing up as the devoted father. But she thought how sad it was that it had come too late.

Suddenly Fran felt very lonely. She had no reason to believe that Rodney would ever really belong to her again.

She heard footsteps – Rodney's – coming down the stairs. The kitchen door opened. Nervously she looked at him, but there was nothing in his expression to suggest that he had been either horrified or mildly distressed by what Peter had told him.

Fran stubbed her cigarette-end on a saucer.

"Well? —"

He straddled his long legs over one of the kitchen stools and said:

"Nothing to be alarmed about. Don't panic."

"But what is it? Why did he run away?"

"Look, Fran – I'd appreciate it if you'd give me that tea you offered just now, before we discuss this."

She had the teapot ready and the kettle boiling. He liked his cup strong, with little milk and three lumps of sugar. She felt really sorry for Rodney. He looked as though he was under a terrific strain.

She poured out her own tea, then sat down at the kitchen table opposite him.

"Now tell me about Peter."

He sipped the tea thirstily.

"You remember when Pete left Prep. School you were asked a few days before whether you wanted him to attend a talk on sex which they generally give the boys who are leaving. I thought it a good thing, but you thought it bad, so he didn't go."

"I didn't —" she began indignantly, then coloured and stopped. "Oh, yes, I remember now. I thought it a pity to open his eyes to all the beastliness when he was still so young and such a nice little boy —"

"And so your 'nice little boy' has now come up against a nasty big boy," interrupted Rodney in a sarcastic voice. "Hence the trouble."

Fran dropped her spoon into the saucer with a clatter.

"Oh, *no*!"

"But, yes. Fortunately Pete confided it all in me. Pretty upset but he's better now because I told him he was not to blame and that Mr. Inholm would agree. I also told him a few other things it was high time he knew. He took it very well."

Fran put a nervous hand to her throat. She felt nauseated.

"Tell me the worst."

"He's had a bit of a shock because he was brought up rather sharply with the fact that all boys are not as decent as he is."

"And? —"

"So he didn't know how to deal with such a crisis. It hit him."

"Who hit him?" asked Fran stupidly.

"Oh, don't be idiotic. I was talking figuratively. There's a boy in the senior house – about seventeen – who took a fancy to Peter's big eyes and long eyelashes, and the fact that he sings like an angel in the choir – and so on. He began to chase him. At first it was only a question of Pete being handed chocolates and patted on the head, but there came the day when this shocker took him down the garden path and told him about sex with a capital S."

"Oh, how *frightful*, Rod! And it's *my* fault. I should have let him be instructed."

"We all make mistakes," said Rodney with an edgy laugh. "Don't take it too hard."

"But this frightful boy – what did he do?"

"Nothing. It was what he *wanted* to do that scared Pete. It appears that there was finally some kind of physical struggle and this boy threatened him, and Pete got frightened and ran home. He just couldn't bring himself to tell Mr. Inholm."

Fran sat still, devastated by the thought that she had been so stupid as to want to preserve her son's innocence. Of course he was scared. *Of course he was.*

She hid her face in her hands.

"It might have been much worse. I feel awful!"

"There's nothing to get so upset about, fortunately," said Rodney in a gruff voice, and went round to her and put a hand against her shoulder.

She jerked away from him. She hadn't meant to do that or to be nasty but deep down inside she was still smarting hideously from the pain of the blows he had inflicted upon her love, and her pride. Now she was smarting because of her own failure with Pete.

Then, immediately (for it was never in Fran's nature to be malicious), she looked up and sobbed:

"Sorry . . . I . . . I'm all over the place."

Rodney sat down again. He did not look at her.

He had felt much closer to his son than usual while he sat upstairs listening to the rather garbled but welcome explanation of Pete's flight from school. Welcome, because it had only taken Rodney a few minutes to realise that Pete had not been seriously involved. He told him he should have gone straight to Mr. Inholm. When Pete said: 'Yes, Dad, I see that now,' in a whisper, Rodney felt extraordinarily sorry for him. Poor kid!

Strangely enough, even while he was up there trying to instruct and comfort his son, Rodney had thought about Perdita, too. The golden girl whose grace and beauty were consigned to the fire, and who was now no more than dust. Not once, but several times she had reproached him because he seemed to take little interest in Peter. Odd, how he had been brought face to face with his failings by *her*.

He turned to his wife.

"There's nothing to worry about any more, Fran," he said, and drew a long sigh and shut his eyes against the hard bright fluorescent light in the ceiling. "He's quite prepared to go back to school."

"Tomorrow, not tonight," said Fran quickly, and got up, went to the cooker and pulled away a saucepan of stock that was boiling over. "I must go down the King's Road and get something for dinner," she added.

"I'll take you both out —" began Rodney.

"No, I couldn't stand it. I'd rather be at home – so would Pete. Wouldn't you?"

"Yes," said Rodney and sighed again.

"Ought I to speak to Pete?" she said.

"No – it will only embarrass him. He just isn't a silly ignorant kid any more – he's grown up. I'm really rather proud of him."

Fran swung round, her eyes brightening.

"Oh, Rod – I'm so glad."

Rodney kicked the table leg.

"Dammit all, you talk as though he belongs to you and not me. He is my son as well, you know. Why shouldn't I be proud of him?"

"Oh, quite!" said Fran in a strangled voice, and went on with her work, then added: "I must dash down to the butcher."

"I'll go for you – just write down what you want."

"But you're tired —" she began.

"Oh, hell, so are you."

She tried not to cry again and made a short list and handed it to him.

"Butcher and baker. We need a loaf, now Pete's home."

"I'll go straight away. And I'll phone the Headmaster when I get back, and have a word with Inholm tomorrow."

"Why tomorrow?"

"I'll see him. I'll take the morning off and drive Pete back. I'd like to talk to Inholm myself. I hope they expel that rat."

Fran was staring at her husband, blinking with surprise.

"*You're* going to take Pete back?"

"Yes, of course. It's my job. I'm not having you go down. You know how self-conscious you get with anything of this sort."

He did not wait for her reply, but walked out of the kitchen, leaving her there, still incredulous.

20

THE following afternoon Fran was doing some ironing when Rodney telephoned, as arranged, from the City. He had promised to do so after leaving Peter at school, then he meant to go straight on to the office.

"Everything's fine, so cheer up," he said.

"What happened?"

"As he told us last night, the Head had already been tipped off about this senior boy who had also annoyed other juniors, and had already asked his parents to remove him. He wasn't there when Peter got back."

"Oh, Rod, what a relief."

"Inholm, himself, was extremely pleasant and sympathetic. I've always thought him a nice type."

"He wasn't furious with Pete for running away?"

"On the contrary – as he said to me when we were alone – delighted that *that* sort of thing repelled our boy. It goes on at most Public Schools and let's face it, it's the ignorant ones who fare worst anyhow. While Pete was still with us, Inholm patted him on the back and told him that next time he had any problems, he was to go to him and not worry his parents. Besides which, he told Peter the staff were in a state when he was found missing and naturally they didn't want a repetition of that. But Inholm promised Pete that there would be no more trouble with the young gentleman they had expelled, and that Pete could get on with his work in peace now."

"How was he when you left him?"

"In good form. Completely changed. It's obvious this thing has been on his mind the last once or twice we've seen him, and it was all building up."

"You've really been very good about this, Rod. Thanks awfully. I couldn't have managed without you."

Even as Fran said those words a hot red spread over the natural pallor of her skin. She was glad when Rodney said he must ring off.

She walked up to his dressing-room – that room in which she had first seen Perdita's photograph, and suffered such utter desolation of heart and soul.

A letter had come this morning from Perdita's aunt. She had sent a rather confused apology for the diary incident. Fran tore it up and decided that this was the end of Mrs. Cornhill.

As she stood staring around Rodney's room, she also remembered how she had come home yesterday and decided to walk out. She was ashamed of herself.

I couldn't have done without you, she had just told Rodney. Too true. And how could Pete do without his father? Ever since Fran learned that Rodney had a mistress she had been trying to keep the family together because of Peter. She had been proved right. Peter had proved it – painfully but clearly. There were times when a boy needed his father and his mother just wouldn't do . . . *and I*, Fran thought with deep remorse, *am not as clever a mother as I thought I was.*

'I can't tell *you*, Mum!' he had kept repeating. Maybe there were many boys who felt less shy – modern, knowing little boys. But Pete was old-fashioned – easily embarrassed.

If Rodney had failed Peter, well – so had she. And if she left Rodney, she would be going back on all her principles and forgetting all she had ever preached, about the evils of divorce when there was a family.

She felt so mixed-up, she thought hopelessly. The truth was, she still loved her husband. But she could not forget that girl, or that diary.

She decided to go and see an old blind lady who had been her mother's governess, and who was now in a Home. Fran visited poor old Miss Osterly at regular intervals. She read to her, which Miss Osterly adored.

This afternoon she talked brightly and cheerfully, and tried to keep her mind off her own problems. As usual Miss Osterly asked after the family.

"How is that dear little boy?"

"Fine! Fine! Not so little any more – growing fast."

"And your sweet husband? Always such a perfect gentleman, your dear Rodney. Although I can't see him these days, I do remember how handsome he looked when you two were married. And so much in love with you, dear."

"Yes," said Fran in a bleak voice, and was glad that Miss Osterly could not see her expression.

Rodney came home looking worse than he had done when he left this morning to drive Peter back to school.

Fran had prepared dinner. She had changed into an attractive blue and silver caftan, which suited her. For the first time for days she had also taken trouble with her hair and make-up. Why, precisely, she did not know. She just felt like it. It was almost like a sort of spiritual convalescence, she thought.

"You aren't ill, are you, Rod?" she asked quite anxiously as she watched him walk to the fire.

"No, only fagged out. Get me a gin, Fran."

"You seem to be tired all the time now. You ought to have a check-up. And a lot of gin won't help, really."

He grinned at her – the sort of grin she hadn't seen on his face for a long time and which she had missed. It had an impish quality and she used to find it very attractive in the old days.

"What are you trying to do?" he asked. "Drive me into a hospital – or a Mental Home, and keep me locked up? I suppose I am a bit round the bend."

"Nonsense. But you used to have such a lot of vitality."

He looked away from her, twirled the stem of his glass and shrugged.

"I'm afraid I'm never on the top of my form these days. I sleep so badly."

"That's certainly new for you. It's your nerves, Rod. I'm

the same. What you need is a long holiday away from – from everything. Me, too."

He looked at her. Suddenly he noticed the small attractive figure in the blue and silver caftan. He made a gesture toward her.

"Why should I want to get away from anybody who looks as nice as you do tonight?"

"Oh, my God, don't be sarcastic," she snapped, and was furious with herself for blushing.

"My dear Fran, I was . . . sincere. You do look exceptionally nice."

"Thanks," she said, and bent down and picked up a carnation that had dropped out of the bowl on the table beside the sofa. Then she looked up at him:

"By the way these arrived this morning. No card. Some unknown admirer."

Rodney looked sheepish.

"As a matter of fact I sent them. I've been rather neglecting you lately and there didn't seem to be any flowers around the house. Pete and I passed a florist and we nipped in."

She stood very still, wondering when she had ever been more pleased.

"That was nice of you, Rod."

"Oh, for God's sake, I'm the reverse of nice and you know it. But I just wanted to show my appreciation. You've been so terribly good to me since – since —" He broke off. She put in quickly:

"Oh, I know you've been surprised I haven't damned your eyes and walked out on you. But after all we did agree we wouldn't break up until Pete left school, and I was only thinking this afternoon how right I was to say that a divorce would upset him – *terribly*. He asked for you as soon as he got home. I was of no importance."

"It was an unusual occasion."

"There are other things he'll need you for in the future."

Rodney sat down. He leaned his head against a cushion, and shut his eyes. Seeing him like this, Fran thought how he had changed. He looked so dreadfully worn.

Fran put down her own glass and cigarette, sat down on the sofa by Rodney, and took one of his hands between her own.

"Ugh! You're frozen, poor old Rod!"

To her surprise he put his arms around her and hid his face against her breast. All the tears she had ever shed seemed as nothing to the bitterness of those that rained down his cheeks and soaked her skin. She was shattered, Rod had never been the sort of man to give way to such weakness. He had never been emotional. But that he was bitterly unhappy now, beyond bearing, was obvious.

She could not feel resentment against him any more. She held him close, smoothing his hair, bending to kiss his hair.

"My poor, poor old Rod."

He did not raise his head but clung to her.

"God Almighty, how can you be sorry for me? You ought to loathe me."

"I just don't."

"I've hurt you so badly. Why don't you hate me?"

"I've tried to but I can't. You're still my husband and Pete's father."

"I'm not fit to be either. I behaved frightfully to you while *she* was alive."

"She's dead. Try not to think about her."

He drew great long sobs, gasping:

"I've been trying, and I will get over it; of course I will. But it only happened the other day. Just give me time."

Fran closed her eyes. This wasn't Rod – her husband, who she was holding to her breast. This was not even a strong man. This was a boy, weak and exhausted by grief, by remorse, by mental and physical conflict. All that was maternal and compassionate in Fran's nature, prompted her to be kind to him.

"Of course you'll get over it," she repeated, "and so will I."

"I don't see how you can. I've done you so much harm."

"Oh, my dear, don't let's exaggerate. Heaps of men are unfaithful to their wives. Some women would say I oughtn't to have made such a fuss about it. But I just happen to be stupidly full of principles and rather sentimental – and I believed in you."

"You're very sweet," he said huskily, released her now, sat up and pulled a handkerchief out and wiped his face. "I do apologise. I've made a fool of myself."

"You haven't, Rod. You're just a bit all-in – that's it."

He picked up his glass again and drained it.

"That's right – I'm all-in."

"And don't," she added, "think that you're the only weak one in this family. I felt so frightful after I'd seen Mrs. Cornhill yesterday that I packed up. I decided to be out of the house before you came back – to fly to Jersey."

Astonished, he stared at her.

"*You* were going to leave *me*?"

"I was."

"Then why didn't you?"

"Because Peter turned up."

"Yes, of course. But why did you suddenly reach the decision to go? After all you'd said about us sticking together until Peter left school."

"Well, there you are, I told you, you weren't the only weak one. I went to pieces. I didn't want to go on. Pretending to be friends during the holidays in front of Peter. Pretending in front of all our friends. Pretending all the time. I didn't think I could bear it."

She stood up, her hands locked together and walked to the fireplace.

"If you want to know the brutal truth, Rod," she added, "it wasn't so much the thought of Perdita, as the way I felt when I found her photograph with Miranda's. That killed me. I realised you probably fell for her because of the daughter you lost. And *I* was to blame."

Rodney also stood up. His hair was untidy, his face red.

"For God's sake, don't keep on with that myth. It isn't true. It's a psychological thing with you. It was a mistake anyone might have made. You only left her for a few minutes. I swear to God I don't hold it against you these days."

"But she looked like Perdita, and you sort of felt you wanted your daughter back *as well as Perdita.*"

"That's carrying things too far."

"It's true. It's true!" she said passionately, and looked up at him with tragic eyes.

He came to her, pulled the small figure into his arms, and pressed his cheek to hers.

"It isn't. You've got to believe it. I was touched by the likeness between them to start with, but at the end, the thought of Miranda rarely entered my head. Look, Fran, we can't go on like this."

She clung to him as he had clung to her, sobbing:

"I know we can't. Even for Peter's sake, we can't."

He moved away from her. She could see his shoulders jerking which only happened when he was in an acute state of nerves. Drying her eyes, she calmed down and spoke quietly.

"Oh, Rod, you and I have got to get away from each other for a bit."

She fancied she saw an almost scared little-boy look in his eyes but ignored it. He asked:

"Why?"

"We can't either of us see straight for the present. Too much has happened to upset the balance between us – don't you agree?"

"I suppose so," he said in a sombre voice, "but you do believe, don't you, that I *don't* hold Miranda's accident against you?"

"Very well, I'll believe it," Fran said, and turned her face away.

"What do you want to do, Fran? Leave me?"

"*You* wanted to leave *me* —" she began, but added quickly: "No, there's no question of us leaving each other. Surely Pete's need for you today has confirmed my belief that a boy does need both his parents."

"Agreed."

"But I still think you and I ought to pack it in for a bit. Our life together here in this house, I mean."

Rodney leaned against the mantelpiece and looked around

the room that Fran had made so beautiful. She had all the taste. He accepted that fact. He had always admired her décor, just as he appreciated her care of him – her cooking. And that thought took him sharply back to the grim remembrance of his dead Love. What *awful* meals she had given him and he had adored her. Poor brilliant unique Perdita! What, he asked himself, would have happened if she had lived? Would America have absorbed her into its gigantic maelstrom? Its fiery furnace of scientists and engineers, consuming them even as they battled for primary position in the new machine-world? The only world that had really interested Perdita. Love – her physical need for him – had taken second place and always would have done. He could never have possessed her mind as well as her body.

Now he was faced with an awkward position. It was too soon after Perdita's death even to try and switch his emotions, his passions over to a woman he had rejected for so long and and once contemplated leaving. Yet he knew in this hour that he was deeply fond of Fran, and all too deeply indebted to her. When he had wept in her arms just now she had generously comforted him. Good God, he thought, hundreds of women in her place might have told him to go to hell and cry there.

Things had changed. *He* had changed.

He had no real wish now to part from Fran even for a short time.

"What do you suggest we do, Fran?" he asked. "I'll fall in with anything you say."

"Well, I still think we must consider Pete's feelings before our own. I'd like us to let him suppose all is well between us and, in fact, much better."

"I'll try to make it so," muttered Rodney.

She had a strong desire to throw herself into his arms and be drawn close to him again, but resisted it. She knew her Rodney. He had lost much of his old arrogance and self-satisfaction. Perdita's death had done *that*. And at the moment he was feeling miserable and rather lost. That was how she, Fran, had been feeling for a much longer time, she thought. She needed breathing space – she wanted to regain the confidence she had lost in her husband, and she wasn't going to get it by reaching too far toward him just now. Later, who knew what might happen?

"Well, I'm quite sure you can't leave the Stock Exchange at the moment," she said, "because you've been telling me that the Market is moving and that you're extra busy."

"That's true, but I suppose I could go and live somewhere else and carry on with my job."

"No, *I'll* go away," she said. "You stay here. You've always said you loathe hotels or staying with friends. I'll ring up Minty and ask her to come for a few weeks. We'll see. She can have Pete's room and you know how she dotes on you. She'll be only too glad to come."

Rodney shrugged his shoulders. He was slipping, he thought; losing his grip. Normally he would have fought tooth and nail to prevent Minty taking over from Fran. Not that she wasn't a nice old thing. A sprightly seventy-something – distant cousin on his mother's side. Miss Minter to give her her proper name. But when he was a small boy she used to come to his old home whenever there was a crisis and take over as cook or bottle-washer. She cooked well, too. Yes, she wouldn't interfere with him, which was something. She was very discreet. But, oh lord — *Minty* every night instead of Fran, who talked intelligently and in the past was so warm-hearted and friendly! *In the past!* It was his fault that that had stopped and she had become frigid and resentful and, at times, hostile.

I've made a proper muck of things, he thought.

"Okay," he said aloud. "Get Minty along."

"I had a note from her a few days ago, actually, asking after her darling Rod. I can get her on the 'phone these days. If there is an emergency, one can ring the woman next door. You know she moved a few months ago to a little flat in Carshalton."

"I believe you did tell me."

"You never remember anything I tell you."

She said this in quite a friendly way, although usually it would have started on argument. Now, suddenly Rodney in his wretched state of mind welcomed the normality and agreed. He *was* forgetful. Then almost humbly, he said:

"I don't want to feel I'm driving you away from the house. I'm the one who ought to clear out."

Fran bent over the fire and pushed a log into place. It sprang into flame. She stared at it miserably. She and Rod liked open fires and had put in this carved pinewood mantelpiece when they took over the house. They both hated electricity. She had to bite her lower lip because it was trembling, but she said in a brisk voice:

"No – it's settled now. You stay and Minty will look after you and I'll go away for a bit. You obviously must be in town to carry on at the office. I think you need it – to keep your mind off . . . off other things."

"But where will you go?"

"Does it matter?"

"Fran, don't be a fool. Of course it matters."

She turned to him, smiling.

"Sorry, I must get out of the habit of being sarcastic."

"I told you some time ago it didn't suit you."

"I'll stop it," she said.

"I still want to know where you are thinking of going."

"What's our financial position?"

"My God, I owe you so much in every way – please, Fran if you're taking a holiday, go where you want, and rely on me for the bills, and don't stint."

"Thank you, Rod. I'll probably nip over to Jersey and spend one week with Aunt Chrissie. But I shan't stay anywhere for long. There are other people I'd like to see and I'll take this chance. One never has time to fit everything in ordinarily. I'll take the car and drive down to St. Mawes. You know I've got an old schoolfriend there – Pat Blaker – you remember Pat? She's got a beautiful house facing the sea and she's very fond of me. But I'll be back after that. Peter's next exeat is in three weeks' time."

Rodney poured himself out a cup of cold coffee. His throat felt dry. He felt strangely like a man reprieved. Fran could very easily have passed a life sentence on him and gone away for good and all. It was a relief to know that she only meant to leave him for two or three weeks.

"When will you go?" he asked.

"As soon as I've got Minty established. I can tell her that you'll be out a lot because I expect you will want to go out with George and the Locks and so on."

"Feeling like I do at the moment, I shan't want to do anything but have my dinner and go to bed."

Fran gave him a fleeting smile, hands in the pockets of her caftan.

"Oh, you'll get over that. I reckon you'll soon feel your old self and be crashing around," she said brightly.

He did not bother to answer. He could not swear that he wouldn't feel better in time and want to go out with his friends. But he did know there wouldn't be any woman in his life. That side of his life was over. He had said so before and slipped – but this time he meant it. He wanted to tell Fran so but couldn't. He said:

"You'll probably sneer at me, but I shall miss you."

"I shall miss you," she said in a changed voice, and walked quickly out of the room.

21

FRAN sat on the window seat of the Blakers' house in St. Mawes reading a letter which had just come from Peter:

"*Dear Mum,*

"*Thanks a lot for the postcard of that little ship coming from Falmouth, jolly nice. Wish I were with you. Can you send me something for me to give my friend Alan for his birthday next week. I think he needs a torch as he lost his. I expect you know about Dad coming down last Sunday to take me out. It was a terrific surprise and we took Alan and had a super lunch. No more now because it's time for Prep.*

Love, Pete."

Fran lifted her eyes from his hurried scrawl written on a piece of lined exercise-book paper. For a moment she stared out at the glorious view. The Blakers' house was built a little way up the hillside. They had a fine view.

It was a cold bleak day, nevertheless visually magnificent. The garden stretched down to the water's edge. Pecuil Creek was grey – like the wings of the strong gulls, wheeling and shrieking around the harbour. To the right she could see the outline of a small steamer coming in from Falmouth. She had always envied Pat being able to live down here in Cornwall with her family. James Blaker was a solicitor in Falmouth. Older than Pat and absolutely charming. They were a very happy family. Fran had had a lovely week with them. Previously there had been the week in the Channel Islands with dear Aunt Chrissie, who was always so peaceful and attentive. Fran felt a hundred per cent better than when she had left London.

Rod had seen her off to Jersey. He insisted on driving her to Gatwick. How he had changed! Somehow he had become so much kinder. But it was as though all the spirit had gone out of him, and that she didn't like. No one would want to see a man with Rod's old vigour and enthusiasms totally crushed. For a long time she carried with her the picture of his white miserable face. And when he had said goodbye he had touched her cheek with his lips and whispered:

"Sorry, Fran. Sorry for everything."

Later on when she thought about it, both in Jersey and down here in Cornwall, it had come as something of a pleasant surprise to her to realise that this was the first time she had been separated for longer than a week from her husband, yet didn't feel in the least anxious as to what he was doing. Suddenly she could trust him again, as she had done in the early years of their marriage. That feeling alone was heartening. And with the raising of her good spirits, there came the feeling of renewed health.

Tomorrow she was going home.

She reflected on the news in Peter's letter. For his father to go down to the school and take him out on a Sunday without being literally *pushed* into doing it was marvellous. That did as much to cheer her as anything. And the first letter she had from Peter after his return from school, following upon that unfortunate episode, had satisfied her that all was well with *him* again. His friend Alan was a nice boy of his own age and in the same House. No need to worry about *that* friendship.

She had also had two letters from Rod. One when she was in Jersey and one down here yesterday.

Rod had never been a good letter writer, so she expected little. In the first he just told her that Minty was doing very well; no trouble at all, and that as the Market was very high, the firm had been exceptionally busy, so he had been glad of a few early nights. He had spent one evening dining at the Club with old George. Another with the Locks because Harriet had begged him to make up a four at Bridge. Fran's absence he had explained away by saying that she hadn't been well and the doctor had recommended a fortnight's complete rest and change of air.

The second letter from Rod had been a good deal shorter and a good deal more satisfactory to Fran.

> "*No news. It'll be so good to get you back. Expect you when I see you. Drive carefully.*
>
> *Love, Rod.*"

Not a passionate love-letter, but that was the last thing she expected. And it was good to know that he looked forward to her return.

When she said goodbye to her friend, Pat Blaker kissed her on both cheeks and said:

"It's been wonderful having you with us and I must say you look *so* much better than you did."

"I feel it," smiled Fran.

Pat was Fran's age but she looked ten years older. Plump, quite matronly in comparison with Fran. She looked at her friend with affection and some concern.

"You were never one to gossip, Frannie, but I've felt that something isn't quite right *chez-vous*. I do hope —"

"Oh, it's all all right now, don't worry," Fran broke in hastily.

"I hope so, darling. Jimmy and I are so fond of you. Give our love to Rod and tell him he must come, too, next time."

But later that day after Fran had gone, Pat told her husband frankly that she was not happy about Fran. She was so attractive still, but so nervy and changed. She was sure there was trouble between Fran and Rodney.

James, with a solicitor's caution, was non-committal, but admitted that he thought Fran a bit subdued and unlike herself.

"Well, I've never thought Rod good enough for her," said Pat. "She's so angelic."

"I don't really know him well. He seemed all right. A lot of charm."

"Too much," said Pat who knew her Rodney. She had stayed with the Griffords in London on several occasions throughout the years. "I wouldn't trust him an inch."

"Do you trust me?" James asked grinning.

"Of course."

"Very unwise. My new typist is as pretty as a picture and has the shortest mini-skirt in Falmouth."

"Oh, don't be so idiotic, Jimmy," said Pat quite crossly. "I really am worried about Fran."

During the long drive between Falmouth and London Fran had time to worry about herself in relation to Rod.

How would he be? That last note had certainly been most friendly, but how would she *really* find him? Would he still be thinking of that girl?

Yesterday she had heard from dear old Minty, announcing that she was leaving a nice chicken-pie all ready for Fran to heat up for their supper on her return and that she had also made some good soup for them. But she wouldn't stay, she said, because she was sure her dear Rod would want his little wife to himself.

Dear sentimental old Minty! But Fran had vowed never to be sarcastic with or about Rod again, and so she tried not to scoff at the implication in those words.

The drive seemed long and there was fog on the Great West Road by the time she got to Chiswick. It was half-past six before she actually parked her car and fitted the key in the lock of her front door.

The light was on in the hall. The rest of the house seemed to be in darkness.

"Rod! Rod, are you there? I'm home!" she called out.

No answer. She felt absurdly disappointed. Surely he might have made an effort to be here to welcome her. He knew perfectly well how long it would take, as she had said she was starting out at eight o'clock this morning. But, of course, if he was all that busy on the Stock Exchange, he might well be delayed.

Fran left her suitcase in the hall. She took off the leather sheepskin-lined coat which she wore for long drives, and switched on the light in the kitchen. Nothing there but a welcoming note from dear Minty and all the dishes and food laid out on the table. Just what one would expect from that elderly treasure. Fran walked into the drawing-room. A few letters and cards for her on the mantelpiece. Two invitations to parties; one to a wedding. She did not bother to open her personal mail. She looked around. There were beautiful early Spring flowers everywhere. She was quite startled by the sight of them. Tulips and forced daffodils, arranged by Minty, who was very good at this. A huge bunch of scarlet carnations in the window. And then when she went upstairs to her bedroom, the first thing she saw was a bowl of her favourite garnet-roses on the dressing-table, reflected in the mirror.

So Rod hadn't forgotten the usual flowers to welcome her. She read the card with it, and a slow warmth seemed to pervade her cold body, and warm her very heart.

"*Darling Fran,*

"*I'll try not to fail you in the future. Just give me time. We must never leave each other.*

Siempre. Rod."

She sat down, holding the note, reading it again and again. A joy that she had not felt for many long weeks and months rushed through her. She untied her hair. Looking in the mirror she saw that her eyes were shining. She had not seen them do that for a long while either.

"*We must never leave each other.*" and "*Siempre*".

That word alone was enough to satisfy her even if she had to wait – to give him the time he asked for before he could be quite himself again.

Then she heard the familiar sound of the front door being opened and slammed and Rod's voice:

"Hullo! Fran! Are you there?"

He had seen her suitcase. Still clutching his letter she ran down the staircase and smiled at him. He didn't look much better than he had done when she left him, she thought, but then it had been no holiday for him.

He caught her by both hands, then hugged her and leaned a cheek against hers.

"Welcome home, Fran. I'm damned pleased to get you back."

"I'm terribly pleased, too, Rod."

"Let's look at you. My word, you're quite brown."

"It's that Cornish wind blowing from the sea. I've done a lot of walking."

"You look simply fine and very charming if I may say so."

"Oh, Rod, thanks." She laughed with embarrassment.

He released her hands and took off his coat. She ran into the drawing-room in front of him and knelt to put a match to the fire. The house was not cold. The central heating was on but they did so like the blaze from those logs.

Oh, how good it all seems, she thought, as she knelt there, coaxing the flames. Her lovely room – the firelight – the knowledge that she was home with Rod and that he seemed pleased to have her back.

They were both a little uneasy with each other as they had their drinks and cigarettes, then dined on Minty's chicken-pie which Fran heated up. She told him all about the Blakers. He told her some of the comic things old Minty had said and done, and of course, they discussed Peter.

"He was in fine form," Rodney told her. "No need to be afraid that other show had any lasting effect. He was as fit as a fiddle and as I expect he's told you, we took his pal, Alan, out to a meal."

"It was terribly nice of you, Rod. He did appreciate it and so do I."

They were back in front of the fire now. Fran poured out coffee. Rodney lit a cigar.

After a moment he said:

"I'm going down to the school more often. I really quite enjoyed it."

"He's an awfully nice little boy," said Fran.

Suddenly Rodney came nearer her, put out a hand and touched her hair.

"He has an awfully nice mother."

For one dreadful moment it was on the tip of her tongue to make a caustic reply. She realised that she hadn't really got over the Perdita affair. And he couldn't have got over it either. It was much too soon. She mumbled:

"Oh, I don't know about that."

He looked down at her without speaking for a moment. It had taken two weeks alone in this house with old Minty for him to realise what it meant to live without Fran. And he hadn't liked it. He had missed her in a dozen ways. He had meant it from the bottom of his heart when he had written on that card "*We must never leave each other*".

Long before Perdita came into his life he and Fran had grown apart and he had felt restless and unsatisfied. During this last fortnight and sometimes in the silence and darkness of the night when he was alone with his thoughts, the ghost of Perdita had entered his room and haunted him. He had seen her clearly in the golden splendour of her youth and beauty, wearing that familiar white bath-robe, full of devilish allure, switching from the heat of passion to the ice-cold of what she called her 'rationalisation'.

Then as the ghost faded, he had turned his face to the pillow as though to shut out any possible further sight. He knew that he wanted no more of her. He could not bear it. In the way that he had shut his little dead daughter out of his life and thought, he wished now to banish Perdita. For that was how he was made, and in the void that was left nothing should enter again – but Fran.

The two of them spent the rest of the evening like a normal married couple, talking about nothing in particular.

At one point, Fran really felt ironically amused at the way the male being could rise above personal disaster with the greatest ease if it meant a successful business venture. She had really begun to wonder whether money wasn't the beginning and end-all of the average businessman's life. She sat flipping through the pages of a *Country Life* which she always took and enjoyed. Rodney was reading the *Financial Times.*

"I say, Fran," he suddenly exclaimed, looking at her over the rim of the paper, "you remember Joe Wilton told me to buy *Western Mining* a few months ago?"

"I think I remember you telling me about it."

"Well, they've been shooting up. I've made quite a profit. Old Joe knows his stuff."

"Which, of course, is why he's a millionaire."

"It's your birthday soon. I must buy you something good., You choose a clip or bracelet or something you'd like and send me the bill. Five hundred quid if you like."

"Gracious!" said Fran.

He looked at her again putting down the paper.

"You don't sound enthusiastic."

"I've never been able to make you understand, Rod, that I'm not jewellery-minded, though I do thank you very, very much."

"Then what would you like?"

It was on the tip of her tongue to answer: '*To be loved and to love.*' But she kept silent. She supposed it would sound 'corny'. Anyhow she couldn't bring herself to say it.

"Don't give me anything. Why don't we invest a bit of money in a cottage in a place like Bosham near the harbour? You like sailing and it would be good for Peter in the holidays."

She had spoken carelessly and immediately realised it. The colour rushed to her face.

All mention of weekend cottages had been tabooed for the last eight years because of that fatal time when they had been on the verge of buying one. The memory of Miranda sprang to her mind. Her spirits went down to zero. It was as though an invisible barrier had fallen between Rodney and herself because of this indiscretion.

To her utter surprise and relief Rodney got up, flicked a log into place and turned a cheerful face to her.

"Do you know I don't think that's a bad idea, Frannie. You could have your jewellery too if you wanted, but if you do, we'll still try and buy a little place between us. I'll use some of that money that I used to allow Mother. It's no damned good keeping it these days. And, as you say, Peter would be better in a place like Bosham in the Easter and summer holidays than in London. You don't like sailing but you could have a garden. You've always wanted one."

Her eyes shone.

"Oh, *Rod*, it would be *super*, wouldn't it?"

He was conscious suddenly of the beauty of those big brown eyes and the delicacy of her wrists and ankles. It had been her eyes and her long lashes and the smallness and fragility of her which had attracted him long ago. Yet he knew that there was quite a steely strength in Fran behind that fragile façade. A strength of mind as well as of body.

He said:

"By the way, I don't know whether you noticed it but there was a card from Nassau from the Wiltons. You know they've got their yacht out there. Old Joe said when he got back in the spring he'd ask us down to Poole as usual."

"You like sailing, don't you, Rod?"

"Yes, but I never do any."

"All the more reason why we should have a cottage in Bosham or some such place, but what about you getting up to town? You've always said you wouldn't commute."

"I've got the Mercedes. I can drive from Bosham to London. Dammit I'm not an old man!"

Fran felt suddenly very happy.

"What fun if we could really do it."

"We will. I'll leave it to you to find the place. You tackle the agents and watch your *Country Life* and see if we can buy a place at a reasonable price. So at least we'll own a country property before the rot sets in in this country."

"I doubt if it ever really will," said Fran loyally.

Rodney put a hand to his mouth and stifled a yawn.

"If you don't mind, I'm going up. I feel sleepy. You must be too after your long drive."

"I can hardly keep my eyes open," she admitted with a laugh.

They stood looking at each other. She felt a bit bewildered. He was being so nice, so friendly, so co-operative, she hardly recognised her difficult husband. She thought:

I suppose I owe all this to that girl's death. Odd to think that I've had to wait for my husband to be unfaithful to me, and for his girl-friend to die, before I got a look in!

Then she censured herself for such thinking. No matter what had brought about the change in Rodney it was so much for the better that she shouldn't complain about its origin.

She suddenly put a hand out and laid it on his shoulder.

"Rod," she said, "I don't want you to think you've got to be . . . to be terribly nice to me because of what's happened. I mean . . ." she stumbled a little over the words . . . "I mean, for instance, you did once say nothing would induce you to have a country place. Are you sure? —"

The muscles of his face tightened but he broke in on this speech quite quietly:

"Quite sure, Fran. I can't explain but I've done a lot of thinking while you were away and everything seems to be falling into place. I can see I've behaved shockingly toward you for a very long time."

"Forget it," she muttered.

"But there's one thing I want to remember and that's Miranda."

"*Rod!*" she exclaimed in a shocked voice.

"Oh, I don't mean in a bad way but a good one. I've been wrong to shut her out of our lives and our memories. If you want to put her photograph in a frame and have it down here – do – I think I'd like to see it, too."

For one terrible moment she wondered whether it was because of that fatal likeness to Perdita that he wanted to see the photograph, but his next words made her feel ashamed of such a suspicion.

He put out his two hands, clasped her shoulders, rocking her very gently to and fro. His face seemed suddenly the face of the Rodney she had once loved so much.

"I don't know how to say this but just keep it in mind. When you feel better about things – I mean – when we both feel better – why shouldn't we try again?"

"You wrote in your note that we must never leave each other. Darling, I'm with you all the way. We never must. Peter needs us – together."

"It isn't only a question of Pete. *We* need each other. *Don't* we?"

She bent her head because the tears were rushing into her eyes.

"We do, of course we do."

"And you *will* forgive me in time?"

She looked up at him with brimming eyes.

"I have. It's all over. Please, please don't let's ever mention it again."

"You're terribly generous," he said and touched her hair with his lips.

"You're being generous to me, too – about Miranda," she whispered.

"I should never have been anything else. And we've both got to learn to talk about her without reservation."

She drew a long long sigh.

"I think this is one of the happiest nights of my life, Rod."

"Poor Frannie – you've had a rotten time lately."

They went up the stairs together with their arms around each other's waists. Not lovers, she thought, but friends; like a devoted old married couple. But the promise of the future seemed to enfold her like warm, strong comforting wings.

When they reached the upper landing Rodney suddenly turned to her and said:

"Good-night, darling, sleep well, and we'll get that cottage."

"I'd adore it," she said. And thought: *Mightn't there even be another Miranda one day? A sister for Peter?*

Rod called to her from his dressing-room after she was in bed.

"Old George wanted me to sell out those Western Mining shares and I wouldn't. I'm always right."

"I'm sure you are!" she called back. Then she turned out her light, put her face against the pillow, and found herself laughing, uncontrollably.

THE END